PRAISE FOR
the cockroach war

'I'm rich! I'm rich and you're not, you poor miserable suckers!'
Dick Cadwallader

'As Commander-in-Chief of the world's largest cockroach
army, I order you to read this book.'
Emma Judge

'It's all true. Especially the bit about the monkey's brains.
And I really am like Hercules, Batman and
Buzz Lightyear, all rolled into one.'
Toby Judge

'This book is horrible! It's outrageous!
It should be banned immediately!
The Royal Society for the Prevention of Cruelty to Cockroaches

'Goo! Bubba-gubba-gubba-goo!'
Beverley Cadwallader

**Jonathan Harlen is 'a master of the
off-the-wall, over-the-top, gross-out story.'**
The Age

Jonathan Harlen lives in Eureka, on the north coast of New South Wales, with his wife Helen and far too many children. He was born in New Zealand and still supports the All Blacks, except when they lose. When not writing, he enjoys taking his squadron of 30 pet cockroaches for a walk.

jonathan harlen

the cockroach war

ALLEN&UNWIN

This edition first published in 2005
First published in Australia by Hodder Headline Austr982 Pty Ltd, 2000

Allen & Unwin
83 Alexander St
Crows Nest NSW 2065
Australia
Phone: (61 2) 8425 0100
Fax: (61 2) 9906 2218
Email: info@allenandunwin.com
Web: www.allenandunwin.com

National Library of Australia
Cataloguing-in-Publication entry:

Harlen, Jonathan, 1963-.
The cockroach war.

ISBN 1 74114 490 6

I. Title.

A823.3

Cover and text design by Ellie Exarchos
Cover illustration by Nathan Jurevicius
Original text design by Wayne Harris
Set in 12/18 pt Goudy by Midland Typesetters, Maryborough
Printed in Australia by Mcpherson's Printing Group

For Joshua, Zoe and Max,
the author's favourite cockroaches

Contents

1

the cadwalladers

Let me introduce you to the worst neighbours you've ever met.

I don't just mean bad neighbours. I mean the WORST. The very worst you can possibly imagine.

Maybe you think the neighbours you have now are bad. Maybe they have loud parties once in a while, and they complain about your dog digging up their garden. Maybe their sixteen-year-old son shoots at your guinea pigs with his air-rifle, and their ninety-eight-year-old grandad chases you up the drive with his walking stick because he thinks you've stolen his last set of false teeth.

Forget it. That's not bad. That's nothing.

Those neighbours of yours are a whole lot nicer than you think.

In fact, they're so nice, I think you owe them an apology. I think you should put down this book right now, run next door, and give them all a big hug. You should plant a big smoochy kiss right on their chomper, so they know exactly how you feel about them, then slip them each a twenty-dollar gift voucher as an early Christmas present, and say this:

'Boy, I'm glad we've got you as neighbours and not the Cadwalladers. Not the Cadwalladers of 390 St Clairs Road, Dagenham. I *can't tell you* how glad I am about that. Compared to the Cadwalladers, you guys are dead-set saints.'

Say all of this with a straight face, as though you mean it. Because you *do* mean it. You really do.

Read on for a while and you'll understand why.

The Cadwalladers.

Even now, a year after these events happened, writing that name sends a shiver shooting down my spine. It makes me so mad I could launch myself into orbit and stay there for the rest of my life, just so I would never, EVER have to see or hear that name again.

The Cadwalladers.

Without a doubt the meanest, nastiest, most revolting neighbours this great country of ours has ever produced.

Dick and Beverly Cadwallader were the parents. Shaun and Ian Cadwallader were the kids. Shaun and Ian were twins, but not identical. Shaun was small and skinny, while Ian was big and fat. They were eleven years old and I'd just turned ten when we moved in next to them, at 388 St Clairs Road, Dagenham, in the winter of 1995.

The strange thing is, we got on really well with them at first. They weren't mean, nasty or revolting at all back then. Two days after we moved in, Beverly Cadwallader baked my mum a cake and brought it over for morning tea. A month later my dad invited the whole Cadwallader family to our place for a barbecue, and I played handball and table tennis with Shaun and Ian for two hours, without a single argument.

We thought they were great. We thought they were a regular suburban Aussie family, just like us.

In fact they *were a* regular suburban Aussie family like us. No better or worse. Just the same.

But then, a year after we moved in, something shocking happened to the Cadwalladers.

Something really, really terrible.

A tragedy.

Dick Cadwallader worked for CityPower. He drove a big truck with a hydraulic crane on the back for digging holes and putting in telegraph poles. He was a happy sort of bloke, always laughing and joking with his kids. He had a thick spiky moustache and a big belly from drinking too much beer. He loved fishing, and most weekends he would drive with Shaun and Ian down to the coast and take them out in his little twelve-foot runabout, the *Marybelle*.

Dick Cadwallader kept the *Marybelle* in his garage next to the family car, a Commodore station wagon.

Both the car and the boat were bright, fire-engine red. Dick loved them. Every time he got back from fishing he would park the car and the boat in the driveway, then unroll the hose and wash all the salt off, very carefully, to make sure his two prized possessions stayed free of rust.

Then after he'd done that he would gut the fish and fillet it, so the Cadwalladers could eat it fresh that night for dinner with home-grown vegetables and home-made chips.

Beverly Cadwallader was even fatter and jollier than her husband. She was one of those huge roly-poly women who burst into a room like a human cyclone, letting loose gales of infectious laughter. She had a big round face and curly black hair and a smile that was so broad it tickled her earlobes.

She was over the top, but over the top in a *nice* way. You couldn't help liking her.

The twins, Shaun and Ian, were all right. They weren't very sporty, and I was mad about all kinds of sport, so we didn't have much in common. But we went to the same school—Dagenham West State School—so we could always have a whinge about the teachers, or about the kids we didn't like.

What Shaun and Ian enjoyed doing most was playing Warhammer, or mucking around with their Star Wars action figures on their bedroom floor, and I got pretty bored with that after a while.

Still, we had some good times with the Cadwalladers. Some very good times.

I can remember a barbecue my dad cooked, for example, about eleven months after we moved to St Clairs Road. This was just before tragedy struck the Cadwalladers and changed them forever.

It was a Sunday afternoon, and the Cadwalladers arrived home without any fish. So it was a good thing Dad saw them arrive and had a chat to Dick Cadwallader over the fence. When he found out about their problem he insisted they come over to our place to share our meal.

Quite by accident, it turned into a great afternoon. Dick Cadwallader kept joking that his wife Beverly had scared all the fish away, and if we didn't watch out she'd scare the steak and the chicken kebabs right off our plates. Dad got out his six-CD Beach Boys boxed set and brought the speakers out onto the verandah so we could listen to every shmaltzy Beach Boys song that was ever written.

Then, about an hour after we'd eaten, we had a game of footy Cadwalladers versus Judges—down in the backyard.

That was the best time of all.

Dad always acted the goat when we played footy. He was a good player—or he used to be—but every time he got the ball he ran the wrong way so my big sister, Emma, and Mum and I had to tackle him. And whenever Shaun or Ian got the ball, they gave it straight to *their* mum, who was the Cadwalladers' star forward. Once she had it, she wrapped it up in her big fat arms, put her head down, let out a bellow like a wounded elephant, and charged.

She was pretty frightening when she ran at you, I can tell you. She made the ground shake. I went to tackle her one time and got hit in the face by one of her enormous breasts. Now, you might think that wouldn't hurt too much, getting bonked on the snoot by a breast, but she was wearing a stiff bra under her shirt and it felt like I'd been clobbered with a water-melon packed full of wet cement.

I went down and stayed down. I saw stars. Everybody laughed so hard that Mrs Cadwallader scored easily. As she came back, cheering and waving the ball above her head, I heard Dad call out to me, '*Watch out for those bosoms, Toby, they're lethal!*'

Yes, we had some good times with the Cadwalladers. And we liked living in Dagenham, on St Clairs Road, too.

Our house wasn't anything fancy, but it suited us just fine. It was plain old brick and tile, like most other houses on the street, but with a really nice garden, and an extra bedroom that Dad turned into a games room for Emma and me. It was close to school and to Dad's work. There was a terrific park just down from our back fence with a creek and all kinds of sports facilities that we could use.

Mum and Dad loved it. After we moved in they would sit on the back verandah in the evenings after dinner, look out at the trees in the park, and talk about how lucky we were to be living in this place after our last house, which wasn't nearly as good.

'This is a top spot, sure enough,' Dad would say.

'Right next to a park, how lucky can you get?' Mum would say.

'A creek just around the corner,' Dad would add.

'Yes, but no mosquitoes.'

'Kids can walk to school.'

'It's sheltered. Doesn't get much wind.'

'Up out of the flood zone.'

'Close to shops.'

'House has got potential. Gets plenty of sun.'

'No traffic noise! Listen! Can't hear a single car!'

'Good neighbours. Don't forget good neighbours. That's very important.'

'Ah-h-h-h-h yes, m'dear.' Dad would lean back in his chair and give Mum's hand a quick squeeze. 'It's a top spot all right, Lou,' he would murmur. 'They're not moving me from here in a hurry.'

'They'll carry both of us out from here in our coffins,' Mum would agree. 'In forty or fifty years' time.'

I loved the place just as much as Mum and Dad did. I loved my bedroom, with its white-carpet floor and big built-in wardrobe. I loved the gnarled old wattle tree just outside the window. I loved the park especially— anytime I wanted I could grab a footy and go over there and kick it around. I could play tennis or swim or go tree-climbing or explore along the banks of the creek. I'd already made good friends at the school, and I'd played a season with the Dagenham Under 12s, and made more friends there as well.

In short, I was happy as a pig in pig-poo, and so was Emma.

Emma was happy for different reasons, though. She was in Year 8, and mad keen on science. She used to go to the park two or three times a week to collect butter-flies. She loved them. Her bedroom was always full of specimens, fluttering around inside huge glass jars.

But then—

Then came that fateful day.

August 23rd, 1996. The day everything went horribly wrong.

The day tragedy struck the Cadwalladers and turned them into the nastiest, meanest, most revolting neighbours this country has ever known.

2

a terrible tragedy

I can hear you now, all of you who are reading this book, scratching your head in puzzlement and wondering:

What's this kid Toby talking about? What on earth happened to the Cadwalladers? What could possibly change a normal, friendly, suburban family into a bunch of cruel, heartless monsters? Is he serious?

Yes, I'm serious. I've never been more serious in all my life.

And I'll tell you what happened to the Cadwalladers.

But brace yourself. It's not what you'd expect.

If you think a semi-trailer crashed through Dick and Beverly Cadwalladers' bedroom, squashed Dick flat as a pancake and left Beverly a quadraplegic in a wheelchair, you're wrong.

If you think a crocodile came up out of the creek and ate Shaun Cadwallader in three quick crunchy mouthfuls while his twin brother Ian stood watching, you're wrong again.

If you think it was *my* fault—if you think I sneaked over one night and drilled holes in the bottom of Dick Cadwalladers' fishing boat, then poured hydrochloric acid over Shaun and Ian's Star Wars action figures—you're wrong a third time.

And if you think one of the Cadwalladers came bursting into our house with an M-16 assault rifle and started shooting people, you've lost the plot totally. In fact I think you need to have an ice-cold glass of water and calm down.

The truth is, nobody shot anybody. Nobody died.

Nobody went to jail.

Nobody got hurt even the slightest bit. Not so much as a skinned knee or a grazed elbow.

But it was a terrible tragedy just the same.

On August 23rd, 1996, the daily *Mirror Sun* newspaper was printed in Sydney as usual. At four o'clock that morning thousands of copies of the *Mirror Sun* were packed into trucks and driven to destinations all over the city.

Some were put up for sale at newsstands. Some were stacked in piles in newsagencies. Some were collected by paperboys and papergirls for home delivery, and thrown over fences into suburban frontyards.

A copy of the *Mirror Sun* was thrown over the Cadwalladers' fence at 6:28 that morning.

Beverly Cadwallader got up at a quarter to seven, as

she always did, and went to brew some coffee for herself and her husband.

She saw the newspaper lying on the steps. She brought it in to the kitchen table. She sat down and picked off the waterproof plastic wrapping as the coffee brewed. Nobody else in the family was awake yet. Dick Cadwallader's alarm went off at 7:20, and Shaun and Ian didn't usually stir until half past.

Beverly Cadwallader spread the newspaper out in front of her. She turned eagerly to the Public Notices section.

The Public Notices section in a newspaper is where the results from all major nation-wide competitions are printed. Beverly Cadwallader wanted very much to read these results.

Beverly loved competitions. She entered in as many as she could. She bought raffle tickets from St Vincent's Hospital to try to win a car. She wrote away to breakfast cereal companies, saying in twenty-five words or less why she loved Cocoa-Crunch Honey-Snap Cheerios, so she could win a trip overseas. She rang up celebrities on television and on radio to try to win a free resort holiday in Queensland, or ten years' supply of Slinkyfit Love-A-Leg pantyhose.

She played the poker machines at the Dagenham RSL Club every Friday evening when she and Dick and the kids went down for a bistro dinner.

She bought Lotto tickets from the newsagent every Monday when she went shopping.

In short, Beverly Cadwallader was a bit of a gambler.

Four months earlier Beverly Cadwallader had seen an ad on TV for something called 'Lotto Of A Lifetime'. This was a special, one-off national lottery, with a prize that doubled every week and kept on doubling until somebody won it.

There was only one prize in Lotto Of A Lifetime. No second or third prize. No consolation prizes if you came close.

The way Lotto Of A Lifetime worked was this. You had to write eight numbers down on a special entry form, and hand that entry form in at your newsagency or at other designated Lotto Of A Lifetime outlets. Then, once a week, a special number-selecting machine at Lotto Of A Lifetime headquarters in downtown Sydney randomly chose eight numbers of its own. If your numbers matched the machine's numbers, first to last, you got the prize money. Every last cent. Winner take all.

The prize money in Lotto Of A Lifetime started at two and a half thousand dollars. This wasn't very much for a prize in a big national lottery. Not many people bought tickets that first week. There was no winner, so the following week the prize money doubled to five thousand.

The next week it doubled to ten thousand. Then to twenty. Then to forty.

A month went by and still the Lotto Of A Lifetime prize money hadn't been claimed.

The prize money doubled to eighty thousand dollars.

It went to a hundred and sixty thousand. To three hundred and twenty thousand.

To six hundred and forty thousand.

Then up over a million.

Suddenly, ten weeks after it started, people all over the country began to get very, very interested in Lotto Of A Lifetime.

The queues at newsagencies grew longer and longer. More and more entry forms were being sold. The week the prize money hit one million, stocks of entry forms ran out for the first time and the government had to print more.

But still, nobody won.

The prize money doubled to two million five hundred and sixty thousand.

Then to five million one hundred and twenty thousand.

Then, almost incredibly, to ten million two hundred and forty thousand—the *biggest cash jackpot ever offered in a lottery in Australia.*

By now everyone was talking about it. The whole country was abuzz with speculation about who was going to win. Even my parents bought a ticket, and neither of them are gamblers at all, except once a year when they both have a flutter on the Melbourne Cup. For them to be interested, I knew it had to be something very special.

A huge number of tickets in Lotto Of A Lifetime were now being sold. In all the major cities, queues at newsagencies stretched halfway around the block. With so many people having a go, it seemed inevitable that somebody would get the combination right and the prize money would finally be claimed.

But it wasn't.

On the fourteenth week the prize money doubled again, to twenty million, four hundred and eighty thousand dollars.

And nobody won it that week either.

The atmosphere around the country grew extremely tense. You could feel it in the air everywhere you went. At school, our teachers sometimes froze and stopped talking to us in the middle of a lesson. They would stand staring at the wall, thinking about what they would do if they won Lotto Of A Lifetime and they never had to put up with a bunch of ratbag Year 6 kids giving them cheek, ever again.

In the workforce, there was a dramatic increase in accidents. Factory workers with Lotto Of A Lifetime tickets kept taking their minds off their work.

A woman in a pasta factory put her hand in the spaghetti-making machine.

A slaughterman in a meatworks zapped another slaughterman with his stun-gun.

Pedestrians walked out in front of cars. Cars veered off the road and hit pedestrians.

An aeroplane pilot took his plane to the wrong airport.

A surgeon in a hospital amputated the wrong leg.

On the Wednesday of the fourteenth week the prime minister of Australia held a special press conference to ask the nation to stay calm. The prize in Lotto Of A Lifetime would soon be claimed, he said. Everything would soon return to normal. The laws of chance suggested very strongly that someone would pick the right numbers that very next week or, at the very latest, the week after.

The prime minister was right. The prize money was claimed the very next week, just as he predicted.

By then the jackpot stood at forty million, nine hundred and sixty thousand dollars.

And I think, by now, you know who won it.

At the kitchen table at 390 St Clairs Road Dagenham, on August 23rd, 1996, Beverly Cadwallader opened her newspaper. She smoothed the pages in front of her with an open palm. She leaned forward, pressed her roly-poly stomach against the edge of the kitchen table, and peered at the column headed 'Competition Results'.

She looked down that column until she reached the box marked 'Lotto Of A Lifetime'.

She looked inside the box, and studied the eight-digit number printed there in bold.

She blinked, wiped her mouth nervously with the back of her hand, and studied it again.

She hadn't written her own eight-digit number down anywhere, because she didn't need to. She'd been using that same number for fourteen straight weeks and she knew it off by heart. It was a combination of her birthday (1-6-8-5-9) and her street address (3-9-0).

The same number that she saw now on the page in front of her.

She leaned back in her chair for a moment and let out a long, calming breath.

'No, this is a mistake,' she muttered to herself. 'It's a misprint. It has to be.'

Despite this, her heart began pounding fiercely. Her throat felt tight, so tight she could hardly breathe. Her hands shook wildly where they rested in front of her against the table.

She looked at the number again.

Carefully, oh so carefully, she checked it. Each digit, one after the other. The first five digits matched her birthdate. The last three digits matched her street number. Her brain told her she couldn't possibly be seeing what she was seeing. But every time she looked, her eyes confirmed it.

She definitely had the winning number.

Holy jumping truckfuls of mayonnaise!!! SHE HAD THE WINNING NUMBER!!!

Beverly Cadwallader pressed both hands hard to the side of her head—and screamed.

3

forty million big ones

It was a catastrophe. Just like I said. A terrible, terrible tragedy.

Beverly Cadwallader had won forty million, nine hundred and sixty thousand dollars.

The Cadwalladers were instant multimillionaires.

Next door, that same morning, we Judges were all awake when Beverly read about her win in the newspaper. Mum and Dad were in the kitchen. Emma and I were in our bedrooms, getting dressed for school. It was a morning just like any other morning in the suburbs.

Until we heard Beverly Cadwallader scream.

Boy, what a scream that was. It made the hair stand straight up on the back of my neck. It was the loudest, most piercing scream I had ever heard.

It sounded like a scream of wild panic. A scream of hysteria and disbelief, bordering on terror. The instant

I heard it, I thought exactly the same thing that everyone else in my family was thinking:

Someone at the Cadwalladers' place is getting murdered.

Dad, being the good neighbour that he is, dropped everything and rushed over to the Cadwalladers' to see if he could help. He sprinted down our drive, whipped around the end of the fence, and raced up the Cadwalladers' drive to the front door.

The door was open, so he ran in. He burst through to the kitchen to find the whole Cadwallader family gathered there, in a state of deep, deep shock.

Beverly Cadwallader was still sitting at the table. She was white as chalk. Her eyes and her mouth were frozen wide open in an expression of stunned surprise, and although she was staring straight at Dad she appeared not to notice him at all.

Shaun and Ian were standing with their backs to the bench, looking at their mother in horror. Dick Cadwallader had the copy of the *Mirror Sun*. He was staring at *that*. A harsh, mad glint of triumph shone in his eyes.

Dad stopped in the doorway. He could tell straightaway that nobody was hurt, but something was definitely wrong because everyone looked half-crazy and nobody said a word to him as he came in.

'Dick? Beverly?' Dad said breathlessly. 'What's happened? What's going on?'

Dick Cadwallader turned to stare at Dad with wild eyes. He lowered his newspaper slowly, then gave a strange, strangled laugh.

'Forty million dollars!' Dick Cadwallader croaked. *'Forty-million-dollars!'*

'Dick?' Dad said in concern. 'Dick, are you all right?'

In a single swift movement, Dick Cadwallader threw his newspaper in the air and seized Dad by the front of his shirt. He began shaking Dad violently back and forth with both hands, laughing and yelling at the top of his voice.

'FORTY MILLION DOLLARS! FORTY MILLION! HA HA HA HA!!! FORTY! WE'VE WON! BEVERLY—SHE—HA HA HA HA!!!! SHE GOT THE NUMBERS! LOTTO OF A LIFETIME! WE WON EVERYTHING! YOU LITTLE BEAUTY!!!'

He let go of Dad just as quickly as he'd grabbed him. Dad staggered back to the door, wary in case Dick tried to attack him again. But Dick was standing perfectly still, blinking slowly, looking dazedly past Dad out through the kitchen window.

'I'll never have to work again!' he said. 'Never have to work! I can have anything! A new boat! A new car! A new set of golf clubs! I've been saving for *years* for new golf clubs! I CAN HAVE ANYTHING I WANT AND NOBODY CAN STOP ME BECAUSE I'M RICH!!! HAHA-HAHA!!! I'M FILTHY ROTTEN STINKING RICH!!!!'

He gave another of his weird, choked-up laughs, then threw his arms up above his head and began capering madly all around the room. He danced over to Shaun and Ian and enveloped them in a crushing hug.

He danced over to his wife (who was still sitting motionless, with her eyes and mouth frozen wide open) and hugged her tightly as well. Then, as Dad watched in astonishment, Dick Cadwallader danced back to where he'd dropped his newspaper, scooped it up off the floor, and began kissing it.

'*MmmmmWUH! MmmmmWUH!*' he slurped, puckering his lips under his moustache and smacking them open with a grunt each time. '*Oh yes! Yes! Mmmm-mmWUH! MmmmmmWUH! MmmmmmWUH!*'

'Steady on there, Dick,' Dad said to him. 'Take it easy now. Take it easy.'

'*Yes yes yes yes YES!!!!*' Dick Cadwallader repeated hoarsely to his copy of the *Mirror Sun*. 'You little beauty! Who wants to be a millionaire, eh? ME, THAT'S WHO! ME, FORTY TIMES OVER, BECAUSE I'M RICH AND I CAN HAVE ANYTHING I WANT! ANYTHING ANYTHING ANYTHING! HAHAHA!!! MMMMWUH!!! MMMWUH!!!! M-M-M-M-W-U-H!!!'

After one last extra-passionate kiss Dick Cadwallader clutched the newspaper tightly to his chest and began dancing with it back and forth across the room. This was too much for Dad. Dad doesn't get put off by much—he's a pretty calm, easy-going sort of bloke usually—but the sight of Dick Cadwallader dancing around the kitchen kissing his morning newspaper really gave him the willies.

'I had to get out of there,' he said to us in a shaky

voice, when he got back home. 'I had to. It was fright-ening. It was like they'd all gone stark raving *mad*.'

'They're just celebrating, aren't they, Pat?' Mum said. 'It isn't every day you win forty million dollars. We'd probably be dancing around the kitchen too.'

'Yes, but not like that.' My father frowned. 'You should have seen it, Lou. The way Beverly just sat there, white as a sheet, without moving. And Dick! Ranting and raving about how rich he was! How he could have anything he wanted! He was like a dog howling at the moon!'

'Not jealous are we, by any chance?' Mum dug Dad in the ribs. 'Go on, admit it! You wish it was *us* that had won that money, and not them!'

'Maybe I am jealous, but that's not the point,' Dad countered. 'There was something wrong about the way they reacted, Lou. That's all I'm saying. Something *very* wrong. That money's not going to be a good thing for the Cadwalladers, I can feel it right down in my bones.'

I listened to all this carefully and quietly. I was looking forward to catching up with Shaun and Ian at school that morning, to talk everything over with them.

But they didn't show.

They didn't turn up at Dagenham West at all that day. Or ever again.

That same afternoon, the real show began.

When I got home at a quarter past four, our street was jam-packed with cars. Vehicles of all shapes and

29

sizes were parked bumper-to-bumper on both sides of the road, lining the kerb for two whole blocks.

As I walked up from the intersection at the bottom of the hill I saw a crowd gathered in the Cadwalladers' frontyard. People were crushed tightly together, pushing and jostling angrily towards the Cadwalladers' front door.

The door was shut, and guarded by a team of security guards in uniform. The guards were standing in a line across the front porch, repelling anyone who tried to climb up the steps.

'Let me in!' someone shouted. 'I'm with Channel Three news!'

'Channel One!' someone else echoed. 'Channel One!'

'I'm with Triple K radio! The name's Fowler! I'm on the list!'

'Let me through, I'm with *Women Only* magazine! We've got an exclusive!'

'QUIE-E-E-E-T!!!!!!!' One of the security guards gave an almighty yell.

Gradually the noise from the crowd subsided. By this time I was at the fence on our side of the boundary, halfway up the drive towards our house. I climbed the fence and stood with my feet perched on one of the crossbeams, so I could get a better view.

'Ladies and gentlemen!' the security guard boomed out. 'Please! Can I have your attention, all of you! I've got a message from inside!'

At this the crowd fell deathly quiet. Eagerly they awaited the security guard's next word.

'As you know, the press conference is due to start at half past!' the security guard continued. 'However I'm sorry to inform you that we have a full house! I repeat, we have a FULL HOUSE, and will NOT BE LETTING ANYONE ELSE IN! For those of you who have missed out, there will be another press conference at ten o'clock tomorrow morning at the Hilton Hotel, where the prize money will be presented by His Excellency the Governor General—'

An angry roar went up from the crowd. They surged forward again, to the bottom of the steps, and were again met by a solid wall of uniformed muscle.

'You can't do that to us!'

'Let us in now!'

'I'm on the list, I paid my money!'

'*Booooooo!*'

Someone threw a rock. A window at the front of the house smashed. A man broke away from the crowd and made a dash down the side of the house, with a security guard in hot pursuit.

A police car arrived and swung into the driveway with its siren howling. Four uniformed policemen leapt out and ran to help the security guards control the crowd. I could hear other sirens sounding off in the distance, as well as the *thunk thunk thunk* of a television helicopter, growing closer and closer.

I heard another noise behind me. Before I could move, Mum grabbed me by the scruff of the neck and hauled me down off the fence.

'Toby!' she snapped angrily. 'What on earth are you doing out here? Come inside this instant!'

'But Mum—'

'But nothing! It's a madhouse out here! You'll get yourself killed!'

I gave up and went inside with her, casting one last longing glance up at the helicopter before she closed the door.

'Honest to goodness!' Mum muttered darkly. 'What a rabble! If this is what winning forty million dollars means, you can keep it!'

She took a deep breath to calm herself. 'How was school today, Tobes? All right?'

'Yeah, good,' I said hastily. 'Mum, the Cadwalladers are giving a press conference at half past four. In their own living room. That's what all the fuss is about—all those people in their yard are reporters trying to get in.'

Mum agreed to let me watch the press conference. We flicked around until we got Channel Four, the channel that always broadcast the Lotto results. It was almost four-thirty by this time. After the ads finished, the Lotto Of A Lifetime logo came up with the usual theme music.

Suddenly the Cadwalladers' living room came on screen. Dick and Beverly Cadwallader too. They were sitting behind a table covered in a white tablecloth.

Next to them stood a short, mouse-faced man in a dark suit.

'Goodness, will you look at Beverly,' Mum murmured. 'She looks dreadful, don't you think? She almost looks like she's in a coma.'

The mouse-faced man in the dark suit stepped forward.

'Quiet please, folks, quiet please,' he said, and blew out cigarette smoke in a billowing blue cloud all around him. 'My name is Mitch Grinderling. Earlier today the Cadwalladers appointed me as their agent. I've got a couple of announcements to make before we get started. Okay?'

He gave everyone in the room an oily, slimy grin. Two gold teeth flashed in his mouth: one at the top on the left, and one at the bottom on the right.

'The Cadwalladers wish it to be known,' Mitch Grinderling said, 'that as of tomorrow, when they receive their winnings, they will be opening an account with the First National Bank, and will henceforth be banking with First National exclusively. They will also be taking out insurance against fraud, theft, embezzlement, fire, flood, pestilence, plague and foot-rot with Statewide Conditional, the most comprehensive insurers in the business.

'Any purchases they make with their winnings will be with a SpendSpree Express Super Platinum Triple-A-Plus Credit Card,' Mitch Grinderling went on, 'while any grocery purchases will in future be made exclusively at Big Markup Supermarkets, home of all things fresh and natural. Mrs Beverly Cadwallader also wishes it to be known that she has just signed a deal with *Women Only* magazine for a series of ten double-page feature articles, to be entitled "My Lucky, Lucky Life".

'And Mr Richard Cadwallader will from this day forward be wearing underpants supplied exclusively from the Macho Jock Leisurewear Company's new Wondergruts range.'

Mitch Grinderling paused and gave another oily, slimy smile. His gold teeth flashed briefly again. He licked his top lip with his tongue.

'And now I'll hand you over to the real stars of the show here today,' he said. 'Ladies and gentlemen, viewers at home, please welcome the most famous, the most celebrated, the most *envied* family in all of Australia, Beverly and Richard Cadwallader!'

Mitch Grinderling stepped aside with a flourish as the camera focused in on Dick and Beverly. There was a brief scattering of applause from the audience in the living room. Beverly Cadwallader didn't so much as twitch. She was still sitting utterly motionless, her glazed face completely blank.

Dick Cadwallader gave her a sharp nudge in the ribs with his elbow. The impact almost knocked her off-balance. She began to slump alarmingly.

Dick caught her by the sleeve of her blouse and tugged her upright. He made sure she was stable, then turned nervously to face the camera.

'Ah, yeah, sorry about that,' he said. 'The wife's a bit camera-shy. The, ah, the first thing I want to say to you today is this.' He cleared his throat. 'Forty million dollars. Forty million, nine hundred and sixty thousand, to be exact. Got a nice ring to it, hasn't it? A *very* nice ring. And let me tell you, it's a ripper feeling to win it. I'm on top of the world right now, and the wife is too, even though she looks like she just sat on a cactus. Bev, can you hear me, darl? I wonder what the poor people are doing right now, eh? *Ha ha ha ha!*'

Dick Cadwallader jabbed his wife in the ribs a second time. She slumped sideways again and would have fallen off her chair if Mitch Grinderling hadn't stepped in quickly to catch her and help Dick prop her up.

'She's just a bit nervous, that's all it is,' Dick explained to the camera. 'Stage fright, y'know. But look, I ah—I really didn't want to say too much today anyway. Apart from that I'm filthy stinking rich, which you all know already. I'm sure you've got better things to do with your time than sit round here listening to me. I sure have— *I'VE GOT FORTY MILLION BUCKS TO SPEND, HAHAHAHAHA!!* And please, if you're in need of a bit of extra cash, or maybe you're after a donation to charity, do feel free to ask. JUST LIKE I'LL FEEL FREE TO TELL YOU TO GO TAKE A RUNNING JUMP IN THE LAKE! EH? FORTY MILLION BIG ONES, HOW'S THAT FEEL, SUCKERS? *HA HA HA HA HA!!!!!! WOOOOO-HOOOOOO!!!!'*

With a crazed whoop of triumph, Dick leapt out of his chair and onto the table. He punched the air several times with his fists, waved his arms wildly at the camera, and began wiggling his hips in a primitive, clumsy dance.

'I'M RICH, I'M RICH, I'M SUPER-SUPER RICH!' he crowed. *'I'M RICH AND YOU'RE NOT, YOU POOR MISERABLE SUCKERS! I'M RI-I-I-I-I-ICH—'*

Mitch Grinderling ran in straightaway with a security guard. They grabbed him by the arms and hauled him down from the table.

Five seconds later he was seated calmly back in his chair, facing the camera.

'Ah, yeah, sorry about that,' he said awkwardly. 'Got carried away there for a second. But I did want to say one more thing. Something on behalf of the wife and meself.'

He sat back in his chair and sniffed thoughtfully. Next to him poor Beverly remained motionless as a corpse. She hadn't moved a muscle since the press conference began.

'Being rich changes a lot of things, obviously,' Dick Cadwallader said. 'But it doesn't change what's in a man's heart. I might be quitting me job, taking early retirement, buying meself a new boat and a new car and some golf clubs and all that caper. I might be doing million-dollar deals through Mr Grinderling here, talking joint ventures and high finance and share portfolios with all the other top movers and shakers in this country. But inside I'm still the same no-frills big-hearted little Aussie battler that I always was, and that's not going to change.

'We Cadwalladers aren't going to be selling up and moving into a bigger and better house in some fancy ritzy-ditz suburb out East,' Dick Cadwallader went on. 'We don't need to. We've got nothing to prove. We're going to be staying put, right here in Dagenham. Right here at 390 St Clairs Road, where we've lived for years and where we belong. Isn't that right, darl? Darl? *Darl!*'

Dick Cadwallader made a lunge for his wife as once again she began to topple off her chair. He caught her by the shirtsleeve, just in time. Then, with a horrible tearing, ripping sound, the shirtsleeve split at the seam. Beverly collapsed to the floor.

'Jeez, come on darl!' Dick pleaded, as he got up and tried to yank her back to her feet. 'Get a grip, eh? We're on national television here!'

Abruptly the broadcast from the Cadwalladers' living room cut out. A commercial for Macho Jock Wondergruts came on instead. Without a word Mum picked up the remote control from the arm of her chair and switched the television off.

'Mum, why'd you do that?' I protested. 'It hasn't finished yet!'

'It's finished as far as I'm concerned,' Mum said sadly. 'I've had enough. More than enough. I'm afraid your father's right, Toby. The Cadwalladers have got in way over their heads.'

Mum sighed and ruffled my hair. She always did that when she was worried—it was much more to comfort *her* than it was to comfort *me*.

'Ah well,' she said, 'it's not really our problem, is it? It wasn't us who won the forty million dollars. And now, my boy, I think it's time you got started on your homework if you want to give your dad a game of table tennis after dinner. Go on, off you go.'

4

grand plans

It wasn't our problem, Mum said. Nothing to do with us. We weren't the ones who'd won the forty million dollars . . .

But Mum could never have guessed just how much of a problem it was going to be.

For a week after Beverly and Dick collected their prize money, they were caught up in a whirlwind of press conferences, magazine interviews and TV appearances. Their photos appeared on the cover of *TV Week*, *Who Weekly*, *Weekend Lifestyle* and *Women Only*. In each of these cover photos Dick was grinning broadly, waving a fistful of hundred-dollar bills, and wearing a bright red sports jacket with glittering gold dollar signs all over it. Beverly, meanwhile, stood next to him doing her familiar impression of a dead fish, her eyes open and blank, and her lips forming a perfect 'O'.

They didn't come back to their house to sleep. The place was dark every night and stayed locked up every morning. Dad reckoned they were all staying in hotels, paid for by their sponsors.

Mum finally caught up with Beverly Cadwallader in the second week after the Cadwalladers won their money. She was out in the back garden, picking mulberries. I was in the driveway out the front, shooting hoops. Beverly's car, an old Toyota hatchback, pulled up in the driveway next door. I noticed that Beverly wasn't driving. Someone else was—a tall, thin woman in a nurse's uniform. Beverly was sitting in the passenger seat, right beside her.

The nurse got out of the car and took a lightweight fold-up wheelchair out of the boot. She unfolded it, then wheeled it round to the passenger side, where she helped Beverly Cadwallader from the car and into the seat.

By this time Mum had joined me. She went over to speak to the nurse and I went with her.

As we walked up the driveway I saw that Beverly had changed. Her face wasn't frozen in a stunned-mullet expression anymore. Her eyes and mouth were moving normally, or so it appeared at first. Then when I got closer I realised that the expression on her face was sort of . . . babylike. *Very* babylike. She was popping her lips and gurgling and making little high-pitched goo-ing and gaa-ing noises in the back of her throat.

'She's undergone a severe regression, I'm afraid,' the nurse explained to us. 'It's post-traumatic shock we're dealing with now. The doctor's assessment is that she currently has a mental age of a little over eighteen months.'

A look of pained concern fixed itself on Mum's face. 'Oh dear,' she said. 'I was worried something like this was going to happen. Is it likely to be permanent?'

'At this stage we don't know,' the nurse said. 'It's impossible to predict which way this kind of thing is likely to go. All we can do is look after her, give her the best care possible, and hope for the best.'

'Yes, yes of course,' Mum murmured, as Beverly gave an especially loud 'Goo!' and slapped her hand on the wheelchair. 'Does she recognise people? Would she know who I am?'

The nurse shrugged. 'Try her. We haven't had much success so far. But maybe you'll be able to jolt her memory.'

Mum slowly crouched down in front of the wheelchair. Beverly Cadwallader didn't seem to recognise her at all. She was happily slapping her chubby, roly-poly hands on the arms of the wheelchair, grinning to herself and gurgling loudly.

'Goo! *Bubbagubba—dubba*—GOO! *Bubbagubba*—'

Mum leant in very close. She waved a hand gently in front of Beverly's face. Beverly frowned, then looked down. She tried to catch hold of Mum's fingers, but couldn't.

'Bev?' Mum said kindly. 'Bev, it's me, Louise, from next door. I've just been picking mulberries, we've got a bumper crop this year. If you want some for jam we've got plenty to spare.'

Beverly Cadwallader blew a spit-bubble out of the corner of her mouth. She jiggled in her seat, gave a loud excited gurgle, and pointed past Mum.

'*Horthie!*' she said.

'Bev, it's me—Louise,' Mum repeated patiently. 'Are you sure you don't want some mulberries? They're lovely.'

'*Horthie!*' Beverly repeated. '*Horthie-goo!*'

'She wants a ride in the wheelchair,' the nurse explained. 'She gets impatient if I don't move her. I'm afraid we'll have to go in.'

Mum stepped back. She stared at Beverly with the same look of pained concern as before.

'The poor thing,' she muttered. 'This is terrible. The poor, poor thing.'

She took my hand, and together we stood and watched as the nurse wheeled Beverly Cadwallader indoors.

The next day the renovation work started on the Cadwalladers' house.

It started, and didn't stop for six weeks.

When I say it didn't stop, I mean exactly that. It went on day and night. The builders worked in shifts around the clock. One team started at seven in the morning and worked till three. Another team started at three and worked till eleven. Then a *third* team arrived at eleven o'clock at night and worked till seven the next morning.

So the hammering and sawing and drilling and beeping and clanging and clunking kept up all night. Every night.

For six whole weeks.

The first day began innocently enough, with the arrival of all the building supplies. I came home from school to find the Cadwalladers' frontyard completely buried under piles of bricks, stacks of timber, pallets of roof tiles, and mountains of sand. I was happy for them when I first saw it. *Great*, I thought. *They're using some of their winnings to give the house a bit of a spruce-up. Good on 'em.*

I wasn't feeling quite so chipper at nine o'clock that night, when a huge explosion rocked our house and shattered the window right next to my bed.

I was just drifting off to sleep when the noise of the explosion hit. I leapt out from under the covers as broken glass flew everywhere, and ran into the hall, screaming. I bumped into Emma, who was also screaming, then I bumped into Mum and Dad, who were racing at full pelt towards the front door to see what was going on.

Dad dashed outside, dressed only in a singlet and undies. He came back a minute later looking completely bewildered.

'They've just blown the house up!' Dad called up to us from the bottom of the steps. 'The house, the garage, everything! It's been levelled! What the hell do they think they're doing!?'

Before any of us could answer he turned around and dashed back up the drive. I went out on the steps with Mum and Emma to watch.

In the glow from our outside light I could see the remains of the Cadwalladers' house. It was nothing more than a pile of rubble now, swirling with dust, and a few twisted bits of wood sticking up. A huge dump truck was backing towards it, drifting ghostlike through the dust haze. A front-end loader was waiting ready to start loading up the rubble as soon as the truck was in place.

Dad vaulted the fence into the Cadwalladers' yard and disappeared. I could hear him having words with one of the workmen, but I couldn't make out what he was saying. Then suddenly the dump truck stopped reversing and its engine cut out. After that I could hear what Dad was saying, no trouble at all.

'You tell him I'll have a piece of him!' he was shouting. 'He better stop this nonsense quick smart! I've got kids over there and they're trying to sleep! D'you hear me? They're trying to sleep!'

A short time later he climbed back over the fence and came staggering back inside. 'They're putting up a whole new house, from scratch!' he said to us breathlessly. 'They're working round the clock and they're going to keep building till it's finished. I told 'em they can't do that. They can't work past seven o'clock at night in a residential area—it's against the law. But they've got special dispensation. Approval from the highest level. Dick must've thrown a bit of money around, bought some influence at council.'

'But isn't he *there?*' Mum said in astonishment. 'Where is he? Where're Beverly and the kids?'

'The whole family's moved out. They're staying in hotels for the duration. All right for *them*, they've got the Macho Jock Leisurewear Company to pay all their bills. But what about us, eh Lou? *What about us?!!*'

None of us got a wink of sleep that night. The dump truck and the front-end loader kept working right through till dawn. Dad spent the whole night pacing back and forth in the living room, muttering to himself and shaking his head, waving Mum away when she tried to bring him more mugs of Milo.

The next day Dad took the day off work to try to track Dick Cadwallader down.

When I staggered home from school at four o'clock I knew straightaway he hadn't had any luck. I found him loading the dishwasher with earmuffs on, peering out the kitchen window at the Cadwalladers' place with red-rimmed, bloodshot eyes.

'You know what I'm going to do to that toe-rag Cadwallader when I find him?' he muttered.

'Now, darling, stay calm,' Mum called from the next room.

'I'm going to rip off his Macho Jock Wondergruts and shove them so far down his throat they'll be poking out his bum,' Dad said. 'And you'll be there to pull them out the other end, won't you, Tobes?'

'You bet,' I said, as I collapsed in a heap on one of the kitchen chairs.

'Tired, mate?' Mum asked me sympathetically as she came in.

'I'm beyond tired,' I groaned. 'I'm flat-out *knackered*. It's bad enough coping with school when I'm wide awake, let alone like this.'

Next door, a bulldozer was driving back and forth, belching plumes of black diesel smoke as it levelled the land. A team of men were working on the flat area where the garage used to be, digging foundations. Two huge pink-and-white concreting trucks were parked a little way up the drive, mixing concrete ready to pour.

'I saw the plans for what Dick Cadwallader is building over there, Tobes,' Dad went on. 'It's a monster. A nine-bedroom, three-storey, thirty-five-square monster. With a swimming pool, a triple garage and a private gym. *And* a three-metre-high reinforced concrete fence, all the way round, to keep out riff-raff like us.'

That night the noise from the building was just as bad as the previous night, if not worse. At midnight all four of us were sitting together in the living room, wide awake, listening to the roar of the heavy machinery, the grumble of the concrete-mixers, the banging of hammers, and the shrieking of the circular saws as they sliced through planks of wood.

'Mum, I've had it, I'm exhausted,' Emma moaned.

'I'm going to go mad if this keeps up. I'll kill myself. I've got to get some *sleep*.'

'Don't worry, tomorrow night you can stay at your nan's,' Mum said. 'You and Toby can both stay until your father sorts this whole thing out and we get some peace and quiet again.'

'I'll sort it out all right,' Dad grumbled, as another shriek from the circular saw jolted him right out of his chair. 'I'll *shoot* the mongrel. Forget about shoving his Wondergruts down his throat. I'll buy a .22 and pop him one, right between his eyes.'

'I think all that money's just gone to his head, that's all,' Mum said kindly. 'He wouldn't do this if he knew how badly it was affecting us. Or if Beverly knew. She'd stop it for sure. If only we could get Dick to come and take a look at what was going on, and see all the noise it's making—'

Dad stopped pacing suddenly. His face brightened. He clapped his hands.

'Of course!' he said. 'That's it! Well done, Lou! You've got it!'

'Have I?' Mum blinked in surprise. 'What've I got?'

'Inspectors!' Dad said. 'Building inspectors! They *will* be coming to take a look! And Dick will be too, you can bet your bottom dollar. He'll want to see the progress for himself, get a first-hand report on everything. I know a bloke who's a building inspector—in fact he's in charge of inspections for the whole of Dagenham. I'll go give him a ring right now.'

'Are you sure, Patrick?' Mum frowned. 'It's after midnight remember?' And as if to emphasise this, she gave an enormous, face-splitting yawn.

'My only chance to talk to Dick is when he's here with an inspector,' Dad replied. 'And the only way I'll know when he's coming is if my mate Allan can find out for me. Yeah, I'm sure.'

Dad made the call from the phone down in the hall. A great clanking and roaring came from next door as another truckful of concrete got poured into the foundations. Amazingly, Emma had fallen asleep, curled up tightly under a blanket on the couch. Mum was sitting in the armchair next to her, yawning and gently stroking Emma's hair.

'I think we'll *all* have to stay at Nan's, if this keeps up,' Mum sighed. 'Isn't it stupid? Driven from our own house, like refugees, all because of Dick Cadwallader. I'm starting to get pretty damn fed up with Dick and his forty million dollars.'

Five minutes later Dad came back. His bleary, bloodshot eyes were shining. He smiled at us grimly.

'Just the stroke of luck we needed,' he said. 'Allan knew the bloke who's doing this job. He gave me his home number and I called him up. He's due to meet Dick here tomorrow afternoon at one o'clock. This'll all be sorted by this time tomorrow, Lou. One way or another. You've got my word.'

5

dickybird here

Neither Emma nor I went to school the next day. We were both too exhausted. The building work stopped briefly between seven in the morning and nine-thirty, when the workmen were waiting on some new machinery to arrive. We both managed to fall asleep for an hour, but we woke up feeling just as tired and weak as before.

Every muscle in our bodies ached. Our heads throbbed. Our vision swam. We were so shaky on our feet that whenever we stood up we were in danger of fainting.

It's amazing how rotten you can feel when you've been deprived of sleep for only two nights.

Mum *did* faint, later in the morning, when she was fixing herself a sandwich. Dad and Emma and I were eating our own sandwiches at the table when we heard a crash. Mum had dropped the plate she was holding and fallen to the floor.

We all leapt up to help her. Broken bits of plate lay everywhere, strewn across the kitchen lino. We got her to a chair, and cleaned up the mess, and after a brief rest she was all right again. But it gave us a terrible fright. And it put Dad in an even angrier mood for his meeting with Dick Cadwallader.

Just before one o'clock, while I was lying on my bed trying to sleep, I heard the sound of a helicopter, Dad heard it too, and staggered into the hall from the bedroom, where he'd been resting with his earmuffs on. As soon as we stepped outside we saw it hovering ten metres above the Cadwalladers' driveway, coming in to land. It wasn't a TV helicopter this time. It was painted bright red, with glittering gold dollar signs emblazoned on it. Across the side of the cockpit, in big gold capital letters, was the inscription: FORTY MILLION BIG ONES! HOW'S THAT FEEL, SUCKERS?

Dad and I fought through a swirl of wind from the chopper blades to the end of our driveway. Mum and Emma were too weak to come with us. They stayed inside.

The chopper landed. Dick Cadwallader got out. He was wearing one of his trademark red sports jackets over a multi-coloured Hawaiian shirt. His trousers and shoes were creamy-white. An enormous gold watch flashed on his wrist. Wrap-around mirror sunglasses glinted brilliantly on his face.

He looked around with a beaming smile, sighed happily, then stepped forward daintily onto the ground.

Immediately a butler stepped out of the helicopter behind him. The butler took out a nailfile and began filing Dick Cadwallader's fingernails. Next came a beautiful blonde woman in a skimpy lycra bodysuit. She scurried forward, holding a hairbrush, and began brushing Dick's hair.

A fourth person—a big beefy man with a beard—stepped out of the helicopter. He was dressed in work-clothes and was carrying an official-looking clip-board. I guessed straightaway that he was the building inspector.

He strode straight past Dick and his two personal assistants, and headed off into the foundations.

It was only then that I noticed how much work had been done on the Cadwalladers' new house. In two days, the progress was amazing. The whole of the Cadwalladers' block had been cleared, except for the building materials, which were still stacked neatly in piles. All the rubbish had been removed. Concrete was everywhere, in thick trenches along the ground and in dozens of chunky square pillars sticking half a metre up in the air.

An enormous hole in the ground had been dug, not far from the inside of our fence. That had to be the site for the swimming pool. Staring at this, I could only gape in astonishment. Dad was right. This place really was going to be a monster.

Dad strode purposefully down the drive. Dick hadn't noticed anything yet. He was strolling forward at a leisurely pace, chest puffed out proudly, a beaming carefree smile lighting up his face.

'Shoes!' he sang out suddenly.

The blonde woman took a sponge-cloth out of her handbag, and leapt forward to clean a spot of dirt off his white shoes.

'Mobile!' he called out next.

The butler reached into his jacket pocket and took out a mobile phone.

'First National Bank!' Dick Cadwallader said to the butler. 'Investments Division! Get me the trading floor, Terence Johnson, and make it snappy!'

Dad arrived on the scene exactly at that moment, and tapped Dick sharply on the arm.

'Hoi, Cadwallader, I want a word with you, mate!' Dad said. 'Right now!'

Dick did not reply. He waved Dad away as if he were shooing off an annoying, pestering fly. The butler handed him the phone and his face lit up.

'TJ!' he exclaimed. 'Yeah! Dickybird here! How are ya? Look, I won't keep you, champ. I was just after the latest on that joint venture in Botswana. Yeah, yeah, the hippo farm. Still a goer is it? Plus the treatment plant for the milk? Excellent. I reckon—WHOA!'

Dick reeled back suddenly as Dad tore the mobile from his hands. In a single, swift movement, Dad spun around and hurled the miniature phone high over the back boundary into the bushes lining the park. He grabbed Dick by the front of the shirt with both hands, and lifted him clear off the ground.

'I said I want a word with you *right now!*' Dad

growled. 'And you are going to listen, or I will really start to get cross! You got that?'

He set Dick Cadwallader gently back down onto the driveway. Dick's face went from white to pink to purple in the space of only a few seconds. He was fuming.

'You've got a nerve, Judge,' he said icily. 'Nobody treats me like that. *Nobody!* Don't you know who I am?'

'Yeah, I know who you are all right,' Dad said. 'You used to be a decent bloke before all this money went to your head. D'you have any idea what it's been like for my family, having this circus going on here round the clock? Louise fainted in the kitchen this morning, she's so exhausted! None of us have slept a wink in three days! I know you've got your special approval from council, and it's all legal and above board, but it's *wrong*, Dick! You can't do this to us! And if you had any shred of common decency left, you'd stop it! Right now!'

Dad's eyes continued to blaze at Dick Cadwallader angrily. Dick regarded Dad thoughtfully for a time, then nodded to himself and chewed at his moustache.

He took a fat brown wallet from his inside jacket pocket and held it up.

'All right, Judge,' he said. 'I know your game. How much to shut you up? Two hundred dollars? Three hundred? Am I getting close or d'you want more?'

'What?' Dad said.

'Go on, tell me. How much?' Dick Cadwallader began plucking out hundred dollar bills from inside his wallet. 'Five hundred? A thousand? Fifteen hundred? Come on Judge, that's more than you earn in two weeks. Buy your family a few meals at McDonald's with that, eh?'

Dad had a new expression on his face now—one I couldn't ever remember seeing before. It wasn't horror, because there was no fear in it. It wasn't surprise. It was an expression of complete and total disgust. Dad looked at Dick Cadwallader exactly as he might've looked at a fat, squirming little maggot that had crawled out of an apple onto his plate.

'I don't want your money, Cadwallader,' he said quietly. 'Strewth. What kind of crawler do you think I am?'

'Take it or leave it. My final offer,' Cadwallader said, and waved the fifteen one-hundred-dollar bills in front of Dad's face again. 'I'm doing you a big favour building here, y'know. Think of the property values. My new house'll raise the whole tone of the neighbour-hood. And when it's finished, if you're a very, *very* good boy, I'll let you come swim in our pool.'

He chuckled, gave Dad a wink, then waved his wad of one-hundred-dollar notes in front of Dad's nose. Dad stood breathing heavily. His disgust was turning back to anger, I could see.

'So you're doing nothing then?' Dad demanded. 'Is that what you're saying? The building work continues? Round the clock? Louise fainting, my kids getting no sleep, all that noise, day and night, sawing and hammering and drilling, trucks coming and going—all that means nothing to you at all?'

'It means fifteen hundred dollars to me, Judge,' Dick said. 'I made you a very generous offer. You refused it. It's not my fault you're a born loser.'

He chuckled to himself again, then slipped his wallet back into his jacket pocket and turned away.

Dad caught up with him in two strides and tapped him on the shoulder.

'You haven't heard my offer yet, Cadwallader,' he said. And as Dick turned around, Dad clocked him one, a real beauty, right on the nose.

6

leaving home

That night Mum and Dad took Emma and me to my grandparents' place across town. All four of us stayed there until the Cadwalladers' new house was finished.

Our grandparents live in a tiny one-bedroom apartment. There's no park next door. I couldn't kick my footy around anywhere. Emma couldn't collect her butterflies. We both missed the trees and the gardens and the sports fields, and mucking round with sticks down at the creek.

Worst of all, it took us an hour and a half on public transport to get to school. Mum sometimes drove us in the mornings, but that still meant we had to catch the bus home. We slept in squeaky, rickety camp beds out in the living room. Sometimes at night Pa snored so loudly it was almost as bad as listening to the Cadwalladers' house being built back home.

A few days after we moved, I woke up to hear Emma crying. I didn't know what the sound was at first.

Emma's no sook, and it had been ages since I'd heard her cry. The night was dark, and although I had no idea what time it was, I could tell it was late. A thick, clammy sweat covered my face and arms, while my thighs felt so hot and sticky under the blankets that they were almost burning.

I heard the noise of Nan's big grandfather clock, *tock-tock-tocking* loudly. I heard the noise of Pa snoring. And above it, the soft, heartbreaking sound of Emma crying to herself, trying not to be heard.

'Em?' I said. 'Em, is that you? Are you all right?'

Mum, who was in the camp bed next to us, sat up quickly.

'Emma?' she said. 'Oh Emma, love. Don't cry.'

'I w-want to g-go h-home,' Emma sobbed. '*I h-hate it here. I can't s-sleep a wink.*'

'I know, I know.' Mum got out of bed and went to hug her. 'None of us can. But we can't go home right now. It's just one of those things.'

'*Wh-why is it one of those things?*' Emma said. '*Why do we have to m-move out and not the C-Cadwalladers? It's just not f-fair!*'

She really started sobbing then. To cap it all off, Mum started crying quietly too. I think it was at that moment that I began to hate Dick Cadwallader. Not just dislike him, but *hate* him. With all my heart.

I think that was when Dad began to hate him too. Dad got a visit from the police the very next day. There would be a court hearing in a few months, the police said, to see if he should stand trial. If the magistrate agreed that he should, and he was found guilty, he might possibly go to jail.

Mum was terribly upset when they got home. But Dad remained cheerful. There was no way anyone would send him to jail, he said. Not for clocking a weasel like Dick Cadwallader on the nose.

'Violence never solved anything, Patrick,' Mum replied stiffly. 'And to think you might end up with a criminal conviction out of this. My own husband, the most decent, law-abiding man in Dagenham. In the whole of Australia, probably. A *criminal*!'

She burst into tears. We all tried to console her, including my grandparents. Two weeks of no sleep, in addition to the stress and anxiety of having to move out of her beloved home, were beginning to tell on her now. They were beginning to tell on all of us, actually. We *all* felt like crying. Even me.

Only Dad refused to accept that we were beaten.

'I'll chain myself to the bulldozers,' he vowed. 'Just like the greenies do, up in the rainforest. That ought to slow the building down a bit.'

'No, don't do that,' Mum replied. 'You'll only get arrested again. Then you'll have *double* the chances of going to jail.'

'All right, I'll go to the newspapers,' Dad said. 'I'll tell them all about how the Judge family got kicked out of home. They ought to be interested in a story like that, surely.'

'But we *weren't* kicked out of home,' Mum said. 'Nobody ordered us to leave. Dick Cadwallader offered you fifteen hundred dollars compensation and you refused it. Not only that, Patrick, but you punched Dick on the nose and broke it in five different places. You've been officially charged with assault and you might go to jail. Do you want *that* reported in the newspapers?'

Dad fell quiet for a while. 'There must be something we can do,' he muttered despondently. 'There's got to be. I can't let Dick Cadwallader get away with treating us like this. It's a flaming outrage, that's what it is.'

Dad brooded over things for the next few days. It dawned on him gradually that he couldn't do anything. Neither could our other neighbours, who were also suffering (although old Mrs Clarkson at 392 wasn't suffering too much because she was stone-deaf). Dick Cadwallader had the money, the power and the influence. We didn't. That was the bottom line.

The six weeks dragged by at a snail's pace. It was the worst six weeks of my life. But finally the day came when we could return home. It was a Saturday, and both Emma and I got up at the crack of dawn to pack our bags. Neither of us had been over to Dagenham at all during our six-week absence. Mum hadn't either. None of us had been able to face going there for a visit, when we'd only have to turn around and leave. Dad had been over a few times, on weekends, to check progress on the Cadwalladers' place and to mow our lawns.

I was so excited as we drove back across town, it was ridiculous. I couldn't have been more excited if we were driving to the airport to get on a plane to Disneyland. This was just a house we were talking about here. A regular house, in a regular suburb, next to a regular park. I'd missed it so much I wanted to kneel down on the ground and kiss the driveway, like the Pope.

When we pulled up in our driveway, however, it was the Cadwalladers' place that caught my attention first. I'd known it was going to be huge, but not *this* huge. It was more like a block of apartments than a house. It towered above every other house in the street. Every inch of the Cadwalladers' block had been swallowed up by it. There was no room for a frontyard or backyard.

All I could see were walls, rooflines, archways, pergolas, balconies—and, of course, the three-metre-high concrete security fence, running all around.

It was red. That was what I noticed next. The whole house was bright fire-engine red, with gold dollar signs painted all over it. There was an Aston Martin Spider parked at the kerb out front painted in exactly the same colours. A helicopter landing pad had been built on the roof, and Dick's helicopter was parked right in the middle of it.

I gaped. This house Dick had built wasn't just a monster. It was *a monstrosity*.

Everything about it was breathtakingly, awesomely ugly.

We got out of our car and stood in front of our modest little house, not sure what to say. It was wonderful to be home again, that was for sure. But we knew in our hearts that nothing would ever be the same.

'Oh, Pat,' Mum whispered to Dad, in a shell-shocked voice. 'It's horrible. It's truly, truly horrible. How are we supposed to get used to living next to *that*?'

'Look on the bright side, Lou,' Dad replied. 'At least it's finished.'

'And at least there's no more building,' Emma said enthusiastically. 'No noise. Everything's nice and quiet.'

'The park's still there, too,' I added. 'He hasn't painted big gold dollar signs over *that*.'

Mum smiled gratefully at us, then yanked a backpack out of the boot and gave it to me to carry in.

'You're all wonderful, you know that?' she said. 'How positive you are. I don't deserve you.'

'You're right,' Dad said teasingly. 'You don't. You better head off back to Nan and Pa's and stay there.'

Mum slapped Dad hard on the arm, then tickled him on the ribs as he leant in to pull out a big suitcase.

'Don't you sass me, Patrick Judge,' she said. 'I know your type.'

'I wouldn't dream of sassing you,' Dad replied. 'It's just true that you don't deserve us, that's all.'

Mum laughed, then threw her arms around him from behind and gave him an enormous hug.

'Oh gosh, Pat,' she said. 'I love you. And you're right, it doesn't matter about Dick Cadwallader's house. It's so-o-o-o-o-o good to be home.'

That Saturday was the first day of the October school holidays. After we'd unpacked, Emma and I headed straight over to the park. I kicked my footy around for a solid hour, while Emma caught two huge yellow butterflies in her butterfly net and took them back inside.

I was out skateboarding around two o'clock when I saw a black car pull up outside the Cadwalladers'. It was a stretch limousine, driven by a chauffeur in a white suit and a peaked white cap. I picked up my skateboard and watched as Shaun and Ian got out the back door with their schoolbags, and waved the chauffeur away.

Shaun and Ian were in full school uniform—long trousers, jacket, tie, hat, the works. I recognised the colours on the uniform immediately. Dark blue, yellow and purple, the colours of Waldorf's, the most expensive, exclusive boys' boarding school in the city.

That was why I hadn't seen Shaun or Ian since the day the Cadwalladers won Lotto Of A Lifetime.

They'd been sent away to boarding school.

And now they were back home again for the holidays.

I decided to go over and say hi. I thought I'd invite them over to my place for a game of table tennis, after they'd settled in. I knew they'd probably want me to play Warhammer with them, and fool around with their Star Wars action figures, but that was okay.

Then, as I got close to them, I overheard what they were saying.

'But we can't, not while we're still living in *this* slum!' Shaun was protesting. 'We can't have *anybody* over! We've got to persuade Dad to sell!'

'He's not gunna sell, idiot!' Ian snapped. 'He's only just built the place!'

'Well he should buy us a holiday house then,' Shaun went on. 'Or an apartment somewhere. Anything to get us away from daggy old Dagenham.'

Ian saw me. He and Shaun turned to give me an unfriendly stare. They both looked so different in that spiffy uniform with the hat angled sharply across their heads. For an instant I had a feeling that I was looking at two complete strangers.

But they were the same old Shaun and Ian underneath, I was sure.

'G'day fellas,' I said, and grinned at them. 'Long time no see. How's it hangin'?'

'Well, look what the cat dragged in,' Ian sneered. 'Toby Judge. The original Dagenham dag.'

I thought he was joking, making a crack like that. I just laughed.

'You don't look so hot yourself in that get-up,' I said to him. 'It's Saturday, mate. You can take off the hat and the tie.'

I reached out and whipped Ian's hat off his head, just to tease him. He snatched it back from me angrily. Both he and Shaun looked so miserable, I couldn't believe it. The first day of holidays, the first day of freedom from their new boarding school, and they both had faces like sour milk.

'Just kidding, just kidding,' I said. 'Hey, I tell you what. This is a pretty decent sort of house your dad's built, eh? Very impressive.'

'It's a lot better than your little rat-hole, if that's what you mean,' Ian said haughtily.

'What?' I said.

'I said it's a lot better than your little rat-hole,' Ian repeated. 'Are you deaf as well as stupid?'

I realised then that he meant it. He wasn't joking when he called our place a rat-hole. He was serious.

'If you think you're coming in with us, Judge, to swim in our pool, think again,' Shaun added. 'You can suck up to us all you like. We've got new friends now. We don't hang out with *westies*.'

They walked to their front gate and pushed an intercom buzzer. A few seconds later the gate clicked open and they went in.

7

party time

That night after dinner I told Dad what Shaun and Ian had said to me. He just laughed.

'Westies!' he said. 'What's wrong with that? Of course you're a westie, Tobes! And I hope you're damn proud of it! You should always be proud of who you are and where you come from. That's part of being a man.'

'And a woman too,' Mum added, looking at Emma.

'Aren't Shaun and Ian westies, then?' Emma asked, puzzled. 'I thought they'd lived here all their lives.'

'They have,' Mum answered. 'They were born in the maternity ward at the Dagenham Hospital.'

'They're westies all right,' Dad said to us. 'They're just pretending they're not. And anyone who has to lie about who they are is a very sad case. All you can do is feel sorry for 'em. Hey, Tobes, you remember the Dagenham footy song that we learnt for the Grand Final last year?'

I grinned at him. 'Sure I do.'

'Come on, then. Up you get. Give your tonsils a workout.'

We got up from our chairs and put an arm round each other's waist. Mum sat looking at us, shaking her head and smiling. Emma groaned and put her hands over her ears.

'Me first, you second,' Dad said. 'One, two—'
And together we sang:

People often ask us!
People often ask us!
Where do we come from!
Where do we come from!
So we tell them!
So we tell them!
We come from Dagenham!
We come from Dagenham!
Pretty little Dagenham!
Pretty little Dagenham!
Lovely little Dagenham!
Lovely little Dagenham!
And if they can't hear us!
And if they can't hear us!
We sing a little louder!
We sing a little louder!—

'No, not again!' Mum begged. 'Please!'

'It's torture!' Emma groaned.

But we sang it again, Dad and me, much louder:

People often ask us!
People often ask us!
Where do we come from!
Where do we come from!
So we tell them!
So we tell them!
We come from Dagenham!
We come from Dagenham!
Pretty little Dagenham!
Pretty little Dagenham!
Lovely little Dagenham!
Lovely little Dagenham!
And if they can't hear us!
If they can't hear us!
THEY REALLY MUST BE DEAF!!!

We yelled the last line. We gave a big cheer, punched the air with our fists, and broke up laughing. We were standing in the middle of our living room, laughing our heads off, when it happened.

Over at the Cadwalladers.

The music started up and the party lights came on.

I'll explain about the party lights first. They weren't regular electric lights, the kind normally found in a house. They were searchlights. They were mounted on top of the Cadwalladers' roof, all around the helipad.

The beam from each of these searchlights was as strong as the beam from a lighthouse. Each one was mounted on a special metal bracket so it could turn and swivel in any direction. There were seven lights in total, each one a different colour: red, yellow, green, orange, blue, purple and white.

Their movements were controlled by a computer somewhere inside the house.

The computer was programmed to let each light swivel at random, in different directions.

If you've ever been to a disco and seen coloured lights flashing across a dance floor, you'll know roughly what I'm talking about. Except that the searchlights mounted around Dick Cadwallader's helipad were a thousand times stronger than disco lights.

Every time one of them swept past our house, it shone brilliantly in through our windows and almost blinded us. It was like we were in a war zone, being bombarded constantly with exploding multicoloured flares.

At exactly the same moment that these lights started up, a drumbeat began thumping so loudly that it shook the very foundations of our house.

Guitars began screeching. Then the voice of Dick Cadwallader's favourite rock star—Elvis Presley— began booming out all around us.

The first blast of music was so loud it shattered the louvred windows in our toilet. We heard a high-pitched *ching*! *ching*! as each pane of glass broke apart, then an almighty *crash*! as the whole lot fell in a heap to the floor.

Mum and Emma leapt to their feet and ran to Dad, who enveloped all three of us in a tight, protective hug.

Some white dust and small pieces of plaster fell on our heads, as a crack appeared in the ceiling, directly above us.

'*What in the name of God is going on, Pat?*' Mum shouted.

'*I don't know but I know who's responsible!*' Dad roared back. '*And this time, I swear, I'll wring his forty-million-dollar neck!*'

He let go of us, then fought his way down the hall through a confusion of brilliant multicoloured flashing lights, and disappeared out the front door.

Mum and Emma and I stood huddled together in the living room. We didn't know where to go or what to do. The crack in our ceiling was slowly getting bigger, dislodging more and more white dust and plaster down onto our heads. The steady *boom-boom* of the drumbeat was rattling all the windows.

A minute later another sound became audible. It was the sound of helicopters. It gradually grew louder and louder. I ran outside in time to see a dozen of them, descending out of the night sky above the Cadwalladers', each one caught in a kaleidoscope of searchlights.

The noise grew ear-splitting as the first helicopter came in to land. The dazzle of lights blazing around the helipad brought water to my eyes. A blast of wind from the helicopter blades hit me and nearly bowled me over.

Mum and Emma fought their way through the wind to join me at the bottom of the steps.

'*Can you see what's going on up there?*' Emma shouted.

'*Dick's throwing a party!*' I shouted back. '*His guests are arriving!*'

'*In helicopters?*' Emma asked in amazement.

'*Sure!*' I said. '*You have pyjama parties! He has helicopter parties! His are just a lot noisier, that's all!*'

'*Snakes alive, the man's totally off his rocker!*' Mum wailed, clutching both of us to her chest and gripping us tightly. '*This is insanity! We can't live next door to this!*'

The helicopter remained on the helipad for no longer than a minute. A group of three passengers got out, then, with a roar like rolling thunder, it soared back into the air.

No sooner had the first helicopter disappeared, when the second helicopter came in to land.

No sooner had the second helicopter disappeared, when the *third* helicopter came in to land.

And so on.

Dad got back just as the sixth helicopter was landing. He didn't speak to us, but strode straight down the hall to the telephone. We followed and stood next to him, straining to hear what he was saying as he spoke loudly to someone on the other end of the line.

'. . . *make a formal complaint, yes . . . 288 St Clairs Road, Dagenham . . . The Chief Superintendent please . . . That's right, the Chief Superintendent . . . No, I don't mind waiting . . . He's what? He's at a party next door to me? But that's what I'm ringing about! The noise here is unbelievable, it's got to be stopped! . . . Sorry? Sorry, what was that? . . . Yeah, I KNOW Dick Cadwallader's got a permit, mate! He's got a permit for everything! He'd have a permit to paint the moon pink and purple if he wanted one! That isn't the point. The point is I live next door to him, I've got the tenth airborne helicopter division coming in to land, and I want someone out here RIGHT NOW to assess the situation and take the appropriate steps! D'you hear me? Hello? D'you hear me? Hello—?'*

Dad held the receiver out in front of him and stared at it. He replaced it with a soft click.

'He hung up on me,' he said to Mum in disbelief, as the roar from the helicopters above us briefly subsided. 'He damn well hung up on me! What's going on, Louise? Where's the justice? What's gone wrong with the world?'

The house began to shake and rattle violently again, as the seventh helicopter—or maybe it was the eighth, I'd lost count by this time—began to lower itself onto the helipad. I saw despair cloud my father's face and defeat dull his eyes, just as they'd been dulled six weeks earlier when the building work began.

I knew then that I would do anything to help Dad beat Dick Cadwallader.

Anything at all.

8

the crisis

Dick's party lasted the whole weekend. The noise of the helicopters landing and taking off again didn't stop until six o'clock Sunday evening. The party music and the lights around the helipad only shut down when the last of the guests had left.

Then, and only then, could we Judges get any sleep.

First thing Monday morning, as I was in my room getting dressed, I heard vehicles pull up outside the Cadwalladers' front gate. Hoping it might be the police come to arrest Dick Cadwallader for disturbing the peace, I ran outside.

Instead of police cars, I saw a line of four bright yellow vans parked at the kerb. On the side of each van, in large black letters, was the sign: SPICK'N' SPAN CLEANING SERVICES—NO MESS TOO LARGE. A team of a dozen men and women in yellow overalls was busily unloading buckets, mops, vacuum cleaners, and other cleaning equipment onto the footpath.

As soon as all the equipment was ready, they picked it up and lugged it quickly in through the front gate.

Just as the last cleaner disappeared, the front gate opened again. Dick Cadwallader came out, dressed in white shorts, white socks and shoes, a white hat, a colourful Hawaiian shirt, and mirror sunglasses.

He was pushing Beverly ahead of him in her wheelchair. The wheelchair had a shade-cover fixed above Beverly's head, to protect her from the sun. It looked for all the world like an enormous pram.

I ducked back behind our fence, and peered out again. Dick had stopped the pram—sorry, wheelchair—and was leaning in underneath the cover. He was speaking to his wife in a slow, clear, patient voice, exactly as if he were talking to a baby.

'We're going for a walk now, Bev,' he said. 'A walk. Can you say that for me? Can you say "walk"?'

'*Ork!*' Beverly said loudly, and slapped her hands against the side of the wheelchair. '*Ork horthie!*'

'Yes, a walk on your horsie,' Dick said, 'to buy some bread down at the shop.'

'*Thop!*' Beverly repeated enthusiastically. '*Wheeeee! Thop horthie ork!*'

'That's right. A walk on your horsie down to the shop. You *are* a clever girl. And would you like a little treat, when we get there?'

'*Yum-m-m!*' Beverly nodded. '*Foggie!*'

'A chocolate froggie? Is that what you'd like?'

'*Yum-m-m-m!*'

'You can have a chocolate froggie, but only if you're good. No tantrums, and no poo-poos. *Especially* no poo-poos in the shop.'

Beverly puffed out her cheeks and made a loud *pfffffffing* noise.

'I mean it, Bev,' Dick went on. 'You do poo-poos in the shop, you don't get a froggie. And I might have to give you a big smack.'

'*Mack!*' Beverly's eyes went wide as saucers. '*Oooooo-ooo! Mack!*'

'A *very* big smack. Right on your bottom. Hurties.'

'*Me no poo-poo thop,*' Beverly promised. '*Thop horthie ork! Foggie!*'

Dick set off again, pushing his wife down the footpath. I watched them till they disappeared. It was strange, but I couldn't bring myself to hate Dick just then. I was still angry at him, and I still wanted to help Mum and Dad beat him any way we could, but it's hard to hate someone you feel sorry for.

And right then I felt sorry for Dick Cadwallader with all my heart.

On Wednesday night Dick threw another party. It wasn't half as big as the party the previous weekend. There were only about a hundred guests this time.

The music was still way too loud, though. All the guests arrived and departed by helicopter, through a whirling, dazzling kaleidoscope of searchlights, just like before.

At breakfast on Thursday morning, Dad was so tired he fell facefirst into his bowl of Cocoa-Crunch Honey-Snap Cheerios.

Dad wasn't on holidays like Emma and me. He hadn't been able to sleep during the day. He had to go to work every morning, parties or no parties.

He was sitting bleary-eyed and unshaven at the table, munching his way slowly through a mouthful of cereal. Suddenly, for no apparent reason, he stopped munching. His jaw went slack. Milk dribbled out of his mouth. His eyes glazed over blankly and his head nodded forward.

Next thing—*whoomp!*—his head landed right smack in the bowl in front of him. Soggy Cocoa-Crunch Honey-Snap Cheerios showered up everywhere, all over Emma and Mum and me.

Emma, who was closest, struggled to lift Dad's head out of the cereal, but he was too heavy.

She'd just got him out when he fell back in again.

Whoomp!

'He's asleep, he's fallen asleep!' Mum exclaimed, as she hurried to help us. 'Quick, before he drowns!'

Working together, the three of us pulled him upright. Milk was running down his cheeks, dripping off his eyelashes and his chin. A cluster of Cocoa-Crunch Honey-Snap Cheerios had got wedged up his nose. More Cocoa-Crunch Honey-Snap Cheerios had got caught in his whiskers and in his hair.

'Dad!' Emma said, and slapped him gently on the face. 'Dad, wake up!'

'*Unnnnnhhhhh—*' Dad groaned.

'Dad, the Dagenham footy song!' I said. 'Give your tonsils a workout! Me first, you second! Ready—?'

'Not now, Toby, not now,' Mum said. 'Stand back, I'll wake him up. I know a trick that never fails.'

She grabbed a pepper-shaker from the middle of the breakfast table and stuck it right under Dad's nose. She quickly transferred it to the other nostril (the one that wasn't clogged with Cocoa-Crunch Honey-Snap Cheerios) but nothing happened. Frowning anxiously, she took a step back and shook pepper all over him. A speckly black cloud settled on Dad's face. It was enough to make a herd of elephants sneeze, but Dad didn't so much as twitch his bottom lip.

'Jeepers,' Mum said. 'That *always* works. It's never failed before now.'

At precisely that moment, a loud, whining, whirring noise started up at the Cadwalladers'.

Instantly Dad's eyes jerked wide open, like a vampire's in a horror movie.

'What's that?' he croaked hoarsely. 'What's that noise?'

'It's the vacuum cleaners, Dad,' I said. 'The Spick-'n'Span cleaning company. They're next door cleaning up after the party.'

Dad stood bolt upright. His chair tumbled back behind him across the floor. He seized a butterknife from the breakfast table and raised it threateningly in front of him.

'I'll kill him!' he muttered. 'I'll kill the mangy flea-bitten mongrel! I'll—'

Some of the pepper that was stuck to Dad's face went up his nose and he sneezed.

'*Yatchoo-o-o-o-o!*'

Mum took him by the arm and tried to calm him. He went to shove her away, but realised what he was doing and stopped immediately.

A look of horrified alarm flashed across his face. He clutched hold of Mum and looked at her in fuzzy bewilderment.

'Lou?' he said. 'Lou, is that you?'

'Yes, it's me, Patrick,' Mum said. 'I'm here. I'm here. It's all right.'

'I'm a mild-mannered man, Lou,' Dad said chokingly. 'I don't ask for much. I've worked for years, paid the mortgage. Fixed the gutters, mowed the lawns. I come home at the end of the day, put my feet up. Have a laugh with my kids, a quiet drink with my wife. I've never hurt anybody. Never ripped anybody off. I'm a decent, solid, law-abiding citizen. So why now? Why me? What have I done to deserve this? *Yatchooo-o-o-o-o!*'

Dad sneezed so hard that he doubled over. He tried to stand up straight again, but his eyes glazed over and rolled slowly back into their sockets. He swayed for a moment, then crashed unconscious onto the kitchen floor.

Mum quickly knelt down beside him. She nodded at Emma and me to indicate he was all right. She didn't try to wake him this time, but left him there to sleep, and got up to address us solemnly.

'This is a crisis, you both know that,' she said. 'Your father has reached the end of his rope. I had hoped that once Dick finished building his house and we moved back here from your grandparents', that things would go back to the way they were before. But they haven't. Things are worse than ever. And as far as I can see, there's nothing we can do to improve them. Your father has done everything humanly possible to stop Dick. I think now we've got to face the fact that we *can't* stop him. He's too rich. He can buy anything or anyone he likes. We're beaten, kids. As terrible as this is for me to admit, we're beaten.'

Tears brimmed over in Mum's eyes. Her bottom lip quivered. Emma and I both rushed in to hug her. She stood with her arms around both of us, her head bowed, and gave a deep, trembling sigh.

'We're left with no choice,' she said in a hushed voice. 'I know we all love this place, and we want to stay here in Dagenham. But I'm afraid we're going to have to sell.'

9

the GX-26

Sell.

Sell the house.

Our house. Our beautiful home at 388 St Clairs Road, Dagenham, where all of us were so very happy.

Maybe you can see now why this was the worst time of all.

The very idea of selling plunged everyone in the Judge family into deep depression. We all loved the house equally, and we each had our own separate reasons why we would miss it terribly.

For two days I wandered around in a trance. On Friday Mum packed me off to a friend's place for the day, hoping that might cheer me up, but all I did was depress my friend's family as well.

Emma locked herself in the garage, where she kept most of her butterflies, and wouldn't come out.

Dad slept on the kitchen floor for thirty-six hours

straight. Mum put a pillow under his head and threw a blanket over him to make him more comfortable.

On Friday morning Mum organised for a real estate agent to come out and value the house.

On Friday evening Dad woke up. He refused point-blank to even *consider* selling the house. He and Mum argued about it all the next day. They were still arguing about it at eight o'clock that evening, when Dick Cadwallader's next party started.

The music. The lights. The helicopters buzzing overhead.

That made three parties in the space of seven days. When was it all going to end?

'*We have to sell, Pat!*' Mum shouted, as she and Dad and I sat with dark glasses on, covering our ears with our hands, in the living room.

'*I'll never let that weasel force me to leave Dagenham!*' Dad replied.

'*We don't have to leave Dagenham!*' Mum argued. '*We can buy another house in Dagenham East! The kids can go to the same schools! There's a good bus service! It'll be fine!*'

'*What about the park?*' Dad exclaimed. '*What about the creek? What about the extension to the verandah, and the second storey we were going to build!*'

Mum looked crushed for a second. With great dignity, she steeled herself and shook her head.

'*Sometimes you have to cut your losses, Pat!*' she said. '*There's no way we can go on living here, and you know it!*'

A wall of noise descended on us suddenly. A

tremendous, earth-shattering, grinding crash split the air. We leapt to our feet, then realised exactly where the sound had come from.

The garage.

Our garage.

Emma was out there with her butterflies.

We tore outside as fast as we could. A horrifying sight met our eyes. A helicopter had crashed straight through the garage roof, destroying the building completely. Bricks, roof tiles, garden tools and twisted pieces of rotor-blade lay everywhere, all over our drive and our frontyard.

Amazingly, the main body of the helicopter was still intact. It had come down directly on top of our car, which was squashed flat as a pancake. As we watched, thunderstruck, the side door of the helicopter cabin slid open and a round-faced, jolly-looking man in a tuxedo and red bow tie stepped out. He dusted himself off, then gave us all a cheerful wave.

'Hello there!' he said in a high, piping voice. 'Jee whillikers, *I am* sorry! Good thing your garage was here to soften the landing, eh? Otherwise I might've been in a spot of bother.'

None of us were listening. We were all looking around desperately for Emma. Mum and I started calling out her name, while Dad ran forward and began searching through the rubble.

Just then Emma came out from behind a tree across the drive.

'It's all right, I'm here!' she called out shakily. 'I was just coming back inside. I missed it by about five seconds.'

Mum rushed to give her a hug. Dad picked his way out of the rubble and advanced slowly on the man with the red bow tie.

'I'd like a word with your pilot, if you wouldn't mind,' he said.

The man gave an embarrassed laugh.

'Well, now,' he said, 'that's an interesting point. Actually I don't have a pilot. This particular model—the GX-26 flies automatically. I punched in all the right coordinates when I left home, I'm sure of it. I just can't think what might've gone wrong.'

He scratched his head in puzzlement, studying the mangled remains of the helicopter's tail. The music from next door had stopped for a few moments, allowing all of us to speak normally.

'You almost killed my daughter, you know that?' Dad said in a choked voice. 'Five seconds you missed her by. *Five seconds!*'

'Now, Patrick, stay calm!' Mum called out to him. 'Remember, violence never solved anything!'

'Get him, Dad!' I shouted. 'Knock his block off!'

'I'll pay for the damage! I'll pay! Don't worry about that!' The man retreated in fright as Dad took another step forward. 'It was just a miscalculation, that's all! A slight programming error! I only missed the helipad by twenty metres!'

'You only missed my daughter by five seconds!' Dad replied.

He leapt towards the man, his hands reaching for his throat. With a lunge, Mum grabbed him just in time and hauled him back.

'Pat!' she said sharply. 'Patrick, stop it! This has gone too far! Enough!'

Dad turned to glare at her with bulging red eyes.

'He nearly killed Emma!' Dad croaked. 'He's flying without a pilot! What's the world coming to? All these idiots running around destroying everything! It's more than a man can stand!'

Mum nodded, still clutching him tightly. She was blinking back tears. I'd never seen her cry as much as she had in the last few days. She was at the end of *her* rope, too, I could see.

'I know, Pat, I know,' she said. 'But it's you I'm worried about, not him. Look at what this is doing to you! You never used to be like this! You've never had a temper, in all the years I've known you! You've never hit anybody! Now you're flying off the handle at the drop of a hat! You're throwing more punches than Mohammed Ali! We've got to sell the house, Pat. It's the only way we can be free of this. Are you listening to me? *We've got to sell!*'

The real estate agent came back to the house late on Sunday afternoon, just as the last of Dick's party guests were leaving.

She brought a contract with her. A very official, serious-looking document with lots of small print. Mum and Dad read it carefully, then signed it.

I'll never forget the expressions on their faces once the real estate agent had gone. It was as if there'd been a death in the family. They were lost. Defeated. All their brave words and actions over recent weeks had come to nothing.

We weren't just retreating. We were surrendering. We were running away with our tails between our legs, for good.

Emma and I went off to our bedrooms, to give Mum and Dad some time alone. I came out a few times to check on them. They always looked exactly the same. Mum sat all evening at the kitchen table with her head in her hands, not moving. She wasn't crying this time. She just sat there, bowed and beaten. Dad sat next to her with his arm around her shoulders, gazing darkly across the room and out the window, at the three-metre-high concrete security fence that surrounded the Cadwalladers'.

The Cadwalladers.

Without a doubt the meanest, nastiest, most revolting neighbours this great country of ours has ever produced.

10

the day of
the hornet

This was my family's darkest hour. Our hour of need. We'd run out of ammo, our backs were pressed to the wall, and the enemy was lining us up in his sights, ready to shoot.

We Judges had never been more desperate or more miserable than this.

It was time for a hero to step forward.

Now, you might be wondering who the hero of this story is. Some of you might be thinking it's me—Toby Judge. Generally speaking *I am* a bit of a hero, there's no doubt about that. Hercules, Batman, Luke Skywalker and Buzz Lightyear all rolled into one. I'm pretty handsome too, in that rugged, legendary hero kind of way (well, except for my big chin, my jugears and my freckles, but we'll forget about those). I reckon I'd look great in a mask and cape. So I could understand if you thought I was the hero of this story.

It would be a perfectly natural conclusion for you to come to.

Unfortunately, in this case, you'd be wrong.

It's not my mum or my dad either. They're heroes to *me*, obviously—especially Dad, who can kick a football fifty metres, eat a Big Mac in three bites, and flip a pancake twice in the air before catching it. But this time it wasn't Dad or Mum who saved the day.

It was Emma.

My dopey big sister Emma and her butterflies. With just a few thousand other creepy-crawlies thrown in.

I'm not telling you a secret when I say that Emma and I were never very close. Everyone knows it. Right from when I was born, when Emma was two and a half years old, there was a distance between us. I didn't hate her or anything like that. She didn't hate me, either. We just weren't close.

If Emma had been more sporty, I would have played with her more often. But she wasn't. She was okay at athletics and made the zone finals for the 100 metres a couple of times. But she didn't love team sports the way I did.

What Emma loved was science.

For her ninth birthday Mum and Dad bought her a microscope. Lots of kids get given microscopes, I know, but Emma actually *used* hers. She smeared all kinds of disgusting substances on those little glass slides so she could study them up close, magnified a few hundred thousand times.

She plucked a hair out of my head once. She scraped some shrivelled dried-up dog's droppings from the footpath. She studied Dad's old fingernail clippings and the dead skin off Mum's feet.

If you reckon *your* brothers and sisters are weird, think about *that*.

I can't remember when Emma started getting interested in insects. I thought it was all pretty boring, so I didn't pay much attention. What I do remember is the day I *stopped* thinking it was boring, which was exactly one week after our parents put our house on the market, when the real estate agent brought some buyers around.

I call that day 'The Day Of The Hornet'. It was the beginning of the end for the Cadwalladers, as you will see.

The Day Of The Hornet began terribly. Emma and I had to spend two hours helping Mum clean up the house, getting it ready for when the buyers arrived at two o'clock. After lunch, when all the cleaning was finished, Emma disappeared into the garage.

The garage had been rebuilt earlier that week. The man with the red bow tie agreed to pay for everything. He bought us a brand new car, too, to replace the old one that he'd squashed flat with his helicopter. So I guess we didn't come out of it too badly.

I didn't feel like doing anything much. I moped around pathetically in the frontyard. A short while later Emma came out and saw me sitting dejectedly on the lawn. She crouched down in front of me and ruffled my hair, exactly like Mum always did.

'Quit it,' I snarled at her. 'Don't *do* that.'

'Cheer up, Tobes,' she said. 'It's not so bad. We'll find another house just as good.'

'No we won't. Not with a park next door, like we've got now. We'll *never* find another house with that.'

'It's not the only park in the world. There are others.'

'Not like this one. This one's the best.'

I was right and she knew it. She didn't say anything for a while.

'Why don't you go ride your skateboard or something?' she asked. 'Take your mind off it. No good sitting here all day.'

'I don't want to ride my skateboard,' I said.

'How about shooting a few hoops? You're getting good at that.'

'If I'm going to shoot anything, I'll shoot *myself*,' I answered, and put two fingers up to my head. '*Pcheuw!*'

Emma frowned at me, then sighed deeply.

'All right then,' she said. 'I probably shouldn't do this, but I've got to snap you out of it somehow. Stay right there.'

She left. When she came back, she was carrying a large plastic bucket half-full of water. In her other hand was a bottle of Princess Pixie bubble bath and a damp washcloth.

'Oh, you're kidding,' I groaned. 'Bubble bath? You're going to show me how to blow bubbles?'

'No, I'm going to show you how to catch a hornet,' Emma replied. 'Stick around, I think you'll find this quite interesting.'

She poured a small glob of the Princess Pixie bubble bath into the water and frothed it up. Soapy, glistening bubbles cascaded over the rim of the bucket and onto the lawn. The bubbles were pink, which was a surprise—although it figured, with a name like Princess Pixie. The colour shimmered and whirled inside each bubble whenever it caught the sun's rays.

'I learnt this trick a few years ago,' Emma explained. 'It only works with Princess Pixie bubble bath. Nothing else. For some reason hornets can't resist it. If there're any flying around within a kilometre, they'll come.'

I didn't believe a word of this, of course. Hornets attracted by pink bubble bath? Yeah, right. And all that green cheese up on the moon must be getting pretty stale and mouldy by now, too.

'You're not serious, are you?' I said. 'You can't be. You're mad.'

'Perfectly serious,' Emma replied. 'Although maybe a little mad as well, yes. All the great scientific geniuses of history were mad.'

'What! You think you're a genius?' I snorted in disbelief. 'Give me a break! A bucket of water and some pink bubble bath doesn't make you a genius. More like a gay window cleaner.'

'*Shhhh!* Did you hear that? Something's coming! Up over there!'

She pointed down the driveway to where the power-lines ran above the road. I listened. I heard nothing at first. But then, as I got used to the silence . . .

A buzzing sound.

Definitely a buzzing sound, growing louder and louder.

'Our first victim,' Emma whispered. 'Excellent. Watch what happens now.'

It was a hornet, I knew that much. I hadn't spotted it yet. I squinted up towards the powerlines, trying to pinpoint where the buzzing was coming from, but I couldn't.

'It's circling, checking things out,' Emma whispered. 'They always do that. But soon the lure of the Princess Pixie will become too much. It will give in to its deepest desires. It will circle closer, ever closer, like a moth drawn to a flickering flame, then—'

'You *are* mad,' I said.

The buzzing suddenly got very loud.

I saw the hornet then. A black speck above the driveway, diving at me, out of the sky.

'It's coming, it's coming!' I yelled. '*Yeow*—!'

I jumped back as the hornet dive-bombed past my nose, straight into the mass of frothy pink bubbles cascading out of the bucket.

Shwoop! Silence again. No noise inside the bucket. Then, after a few more seconds—a muffled, angry buzzing.

'Got you!' Emma breathed. 'You're mine now, my lovely!' She knelt down beside the bucket and spread the damp cloth out over her hand.

'Come to Mama! Com-m-m-me to Mama! Tha-a-a-at's it.'

She lowered the cloth gently. The bubbles in the bucket shook violently as the hornet struggled to get free. Emma's hand disappeared into the pink suds. Suddenly she lunged. Bubbles and water slopped everywhere. Emma whipped the cloth back out of the bucket again, and scrunched it tightly between two hands.

She had it.

I could hear it buzzing madly, inside its new prison. She gave me a proud, self-satisfied grin.

'Wow, that's great!' I stepped in closer, but not too close. 'Can I see it?'

'Sure, hang on a second. I'll show you its head.'

Expertly, Emma peeled back layers of the washcloth with her fingers, until the hornet's head and antennae appeared. The antennae were black and shiny, and waving furiously.

'Hey, yeah!' I laughed. 'This is cool, you know that?'

'You ain't seen nothing yet,' Emma grinned at me. 'Come in the garage, little brother. I'll show you something *really* cool.'

Just as we opened the garage door, a car pulled into the driveway. It was the real estate agent's car. She had brought two passengers, a middle-aged man and a woman. They drove right by us, nearly knocking over Emma's bucket, which we'd left on the drive.

'Oh, no!' I groaned. 'It's the buyers! What do we do now?'

'They haven't bought the place yet, remember,' Emma said. 'They're just looking.'

'I heard Mum say they were really interested. They're pretty close to making an offer. We've got to do something, Em. We can't just let Mum and Dad *lose* like this.'

Emma grabbed me by the shirt and hauled me into the garage.

'There's nothing we can do,' she said. 'It's out of our control. Now come on. I'm about to show you the greatest secret of my life. Something that will revolutionise the field of entomology and make me as famous as Leonardo da Vinci. The least you could do is pay attention.'

She was doing all of this to cheer me up, I realised. It was nice of her. I gave her a crooked, one-sided grin.

'Sure,' I said. Then I added, 'What's entomology?'

'Insect science,' Emma said. 'That's my field of expertise. In particular, the workings of the insect's brain.'

She held the hornet up between us and peered closely at its waving antennae. Then she shut the door of the garage.

'I didn't think insects *had* a brain, I said.

'Not like ours they don't,' Emma replied. 'They

have a mass of nerves in their head called a ganglion. Very primitive, yet very effective. And I've found a way of controlling this mass of nerves without using dangerous chemicals. I've found a way of sending messages to insects, so I can tell them what to do.'

I stared at her, dumbfounded. It sounded like gobbledegook. Yet, after her trick with the pink bubble bath, I was ready to believe anything.

'You can *talk to insects?*' I said.

'Not talk to them,' Emma corrected me. 'Direct them. Pilot them. Steer them like a remote-controlled car. Look, I'll show you.'

We'd reached the workbench. It was clear except for two large glass jars containing four butterflies. Most of Emma's collection had been wiped out when the helicopter crashed into the garage a week earlier.

'The hard part,' Emma went on, 'has been to work out which part of an insect's brain controls what function. Movement, for example. Reproduction, eyesight. They're all separate, determined by a localised bunch of nerves. And that's why I've always worked with big insects—butterflies and hornets, for example. Bees and march flies are good too, because their nerve centres are bigger and much easier to experiment on. Here, hold this.'

She gave me the hornet, still wrapped up tight in the washcloth, and reached up to a shelf behind the workbench. She brought down a small cordless drill. It was just like the cordless drill my dad used to fix stuff around the house, except the drill-bit was tiny, only a millimetre wide.

She pressed the trigger of the drill to test it. The motor whirred smoothly, turning the drill-bit at high speed.

'You're not going to hurt the hornet, are you?' I asked.

'No, no, of course not,' Emma reassured me. 'I'm just going to drill a hole in its head, that's all.'

'*What?*' I jerked the hornet away from her hurriedly. '*A hole in its head? Are you kidding?*'

'Just a little hole. It won't feel a thing, I promise!'

'Like hell it won't!' I clutched the hornet protectively to my chest. 'You can't drill a hole in something's head without it feeling it! You'll *kill* it!'

Emma looked at me sadly, disappointed that any brother of hers could be so ignorant. She shook her head.

'I'm drilling through its exoskeleton,' she explained patiently. 'No nerves. It's just like cutting off a fingernail. The hornet won't even notice.'

'But—what about its brain? Or its gangli-whatever-it-was? What if you drill into that?'

'I won't. I drill down to it, but then I stop. It's no big deal, Tobes, I've done this dozens of times. And besides, it's all in the name of science.'

Yeah, right, I thought. *That's why scientists are the bad guys in nearly every horror movie I've ever watched.*

'You better not hurt it,' I warned her. 'You better not, that's all.'

'Toby, how sweet. I didn't know you cared.'

She took the hornet from me and held it steady. With her other hand she brought the cordless drill up in front of its head and aimed right between its eyes. She moved the point of the drill till it was touching the hornet's forehead. Then, so slowly it was almost painful, she adjusted the angle of the shaft.

'Proto-cerebrum . . . deuto-cerebrum . . . corpus cardiacum . . . There, that should do it. One . . . two . . . *three*—'

With a quick, well-practised thrust, she drilled into the hornet's head and back out again.

It was done.

The hornet buzzed quietly inside the washcloth, waving its antennae briskly, as if nothing had happened.

'Perfect!' Emma breathed. 'Now listen, Tobes. There's a big cardboard box under the bench here. It's the one from a computer shop, filled with microchips. You want to bring it up?'

I found the box and lifted it up to the bench. Inside it were thousands of tiny silicon chips. There were so many I couldn't begin to count them. Each one was no bigger than the tip of a ball-point pen.

'Wow!' I said. Where'd you get these?'

'They're worthless, actually,' Emma said. 'They were going to be chucked out, they're so outmoded. I picked up the whole boxful for ten bucks from a computer shop in town.'

She took one of the microchips and turned it over in her fingers. Then, before I knew what was happening, she dropped it neatly inside the hole in the hornet's head. When that was done she reached for a tube of superglue on the shelf and glued the top of the hole over with a single dollop.

'The interesting thing about these microchips,' she said, 'is that they also contain a radio receiver. They pick up radio signals and convert them into short pulses of electric current. If I place one in exactly the right spot, up against the outer nerve wall of the ganglion, I can control the insect's movements. The pulses of electricity override its own primitive instincts. I can steer it just like a remote-controlled plane.'

She shook the washcloth gently, allowing the hornet to tumble out onto the bench. It got to its feet and stretched out its crumpled wings. Then, with a loud triumphant buzz, it took to the air.

'You might think I'm letting it get away,' she said, as the hornet headed straight for the nearest window and began knocking itself against the glass. 'But I'm not. Watch this.'

She opened a cupboard next to the bench. From a drawer inside, she took out a remote-control handset, equipped with a trigger underneath to control speed, and a knob on the side to control direction.

'Standard Tandy Electronics six-band remote,' she said. 'I've got lots of these. The frequency's already pre-set to 27 megahertz. The superglue should be dry by now. Why don't you give it a go?'

She gave the handset to me. I stared at it dumbly. The hornet was still battering itself against the window pane off to my left.

'What d'you want me to do with this?' I asked.

'Steer, of course!' Emma replied. 'Hit the trigger! See how fast it'll go! Don't just stand there like a dummy!'

I turned to face the hornet. I braced myself. Surely it wasn't possible to steer a living creature like this, as if it were a machine.

Carefully—oh so carefully—I turned the knob on the handset to the right.

The hornet veered sharply to the right. It hit the side frame of the window and fell stunned onto the sill.

I turned the knob on the handset to the left.

The insect immediately flew left, into the other frame of the window. Once again it fell down stunned. I waited for it to get to its feet, then tilted the handset upwards, squeezing the trigger slightly at the same time.

The hornet shot straight up and hit the top frame of the window. For the third time it fell down dizzily. This time it looked hurt. It lay on its back for a while, quivering.

'Can't you do anything except crash it?' Emma asked. 'You're hopeless!'

'Where's the reverse on this thing?' I replied.

'There is no reverse. Wait till it moves free of the window. I'll open the roll-a-door so we can take it outside.'

I watched the hornet carefully while Emma opened the roll-a-door. I was starting to get excited now. Here I was, Toby Judge, of 388 St Clairs Road, Dagenham, piloting the world's first remote-controlled insect. Well, maybe not the world's first—Emma had done this before, she said—but one of the first. And I was only the second person ever to have done it. When the chapter on remote-controlled insects came to be written in the history books, my name would be up there right next to hers.

'This is fantastic, Em,' I said. 'You really *are* a genius.'

'Of course,' Emma replied. 'But just remember that it's a secret. Nobody else knows about this yet, and it has to stay that way until I've worked out all the possibilities. Okay?'

'My lips are sealed,' I promised. 'Hey, hang on, it's flying off—'

I hit the trigger and twisted the knob wildly as the hornet headed for the open door. It veered left at the speed of a bullet and smashed headlong into the brick wall behind the car.

'Be gentle with it!' Emma roared. 'Those controls are sensitive! Here, give me that!'

She snatched the handset from me and went to look at the hornet. It was lying motionless on the floor of the garage, beside the car.

'I haven't killed it, have I?' I said glumly.

'Probably. This isn't a video game, Tobes. These things are *real*.'

The hornet's wings twitched slightly. It rolled onto its side and got groggily to its feet. I breathed a huge sigh of relief.

'It's alive,' I said. 'Thank God for that.'

'No thanks to you, bonehead,' Emma said. '*I'll* do the driving from now on, if you don't mind.'

While we were waiting for the hornet to recover, the front door of the house opened.

The real estate agent came out, followed by Mum and Dad and the two buyers.

They walked to the real estate agent's car and stood talking. We couldn't hear everything they were saying, but we could hear enough.

They were talking about selling the house. *Soon.*

'So that's definitely a firm offer and it's there for you to consider,' the real estate agent was saying. 'I know it's not quite what you wanted, but it's close. *Very* close. If I were you I'd think about it very carefully.'

Dad said something about how they were hoping for a little bit more. But they would consider it, he promised. He asked the buyers how long it would take to get the money ready. I didn't catch what the buyers said in reply.

The five of them stood talking finances for a while.

The hornet, meantime, had recovered completely. Emma had it doing loop-the-loops and figure-eights inside the garage.

Suddenly I got an idea.

'Emma!' I said urgently. 'Can you steer the hornet onto those two buyers? And make it sting them? That might put them off buying the house!'

Emma took her finger off the trigger. She looked at me first in puzzlement, then in delight. The hornet stopped looping-the-loop and flew dizzily out the door.

'Quick!' I said. 'They'll be getting into the car any second! I'll go first and you send the hornet after me!'

Emma nodded. She hit the trigger again and twiddled with the knob to bring the hornet back under control.

I took off as fast I could, sprinting flat out down the drive towards the house.

'*Hornets' ne-e-e-est!*' I yelled. '*Hornets everywhere! They'll sting you, they'll sting you! Ahhhhhhhhh!!!!!*'

I reached the real estate agent's car and hurled myself across the bonnet. As I hit the ground on the other side I heard Mum say, 'Toby! Toby, what are you—?' and then the real estate agent screamed. The hornet hit her in the neck and stung her furiously. The very next second it attacked the two buyers. It stung the man on the cheek and the woman on the nose. It stung the man a second time on the ear. All three of them were screaming now, so loudly I could hardly hear my own shouts.

'*Hornets' nest! Ahhhhhhh! Thousands of 'em! Run for your lives!*'

The real estate agent dived into her car. The two buyers scrambled in after her. Without a word to my parents they roared away down the drive. I turned to see Emma standing innocently next to a tree opposite the garage. There was no sign of her remote-control handset. The hornet had flown off into the sky and disappeared.

'What the hell—?' Dad said. 'Toby! Toby, what's going on?'

'Hornets!' I said. 'They were everywhere! Didn't you see 'em?'

'No I didn't, as a matter of fact,' Dad said.

'I saw *one*,' Mum said. 'But it didn't come anywhere near me. It didn't sting your father, either. Only those other three.'

'Wow,' I said. 'What a coincidence, eh? I'd say you just had a lucky escape.'

Mum and Dad frowned at me. I smiled at them innocently. They were both too confused to accuse me of anything. Besides, what could they accuse me of exactly? There was no way they could know I'd planned the whole thing. And I wasn't lying, because there really had been a hornet. Maybe not thousands of them, as I'd told the buyers, but I was allowed to exaggerate a little, wasn't I?

My parents kept on frowning.

I kept on smiling innocently.

Thanks to Emma's wonderful new remote-controlled insect technology, she and I had committed the perfect crime.

11

cockroaches!

Next morning Dad got up at dawn and spent an hour looking for hornets' nests out in the yard. He climbed trees, inspected the ceiling inside the garage, and clomped around on the roof.

He wasn't in a good mood when he left for work. When he got home again that evening, he called everyone into the living room for a family conference.

Emma and I sat on the couch. Mum sat in the armchair. Dad paced back and forth on the rug.

'Sabotage!' he said to us. 'That's what it was, pure and simple! There is not one single hornets' nest around our house anywhere! Not in the roof, not in the trees! Nowhere! I don't know how you did it, Toby—I don't know how you scared away those buyers—but I know you did it. And I've got to say I'm disappointed in you, son. Very disappointed. I thought you would've known better.'

He stopped pacing and glared at me. I glared back at him defiantly.

'I'm *glad* I scared away those buyers,' I said. 'I think it's wrong for us to sell. The Cadwalladers are the ones who should sell. They're the ones who've caused all the problems.'

Mum looked at Dad anxiously, but he only nodded and smiled.

'Right,' he said. 'I see. The Cadwalladers should sell. And just how do you propose to make them do that?'

'I don't know.'

'You don't know,' Dad echoed. 'Well, mate, join the club, because I don't know either. Your mum doesn't know. Emma doesn't know. *None* of us know. And meanwhile—somehow—you've managed to ruin our best chance of getting out of here with dignity. We've *lost*, Toby! We've lost the war with the Cadwalladers and we've got to accept that! And next time we have buyers in here I don't want you pulling stupid stunts like you did yesterday, because it *does—not—help!*'

I discussed the situation with Emma later that evening, out in the garage.

'There has to be some way we can use your insects against the Cadwalladers,' I said. 'If we can scare the buyers off, maybe we could scare the Cadwalladers off too.'

'Maybe,' Emma agreed. 'But it's not enough just to *scare* the Cadwalladers. We have to make them sell their house, before Mum and Dad sell ours. And that'll take a lot more than one hornet.'

'How many hornets could we catch, then? Fifty? A hundred? A hundred would be enough, don't you reckon?'

Emma shook her head. 'No way we could catch that many. Not unless we find some really huge nests. I've had the bubble bath out for hours sometimes and I haven't got any at all.'

I paused for a moment, considering this. I'd never seen or heard of hornets' nests in Dagenham. They had to be somewhere—otherwise there wouldn't be any hornets flying around—but where?

'Maybe we could ring a pest exterminator,' I suggested. 'We could get him to tell us when he finds one. Then we could go out with the drill, put microchips in their heads, and fly them all back.'

Emma shook her head again. 'No, it's not worth it. It would take us months to get enough to make a strike force. And besides, all the Cadwalladers have to do is close their windows and doors and we can't get at them. We need a different insect, one that can go anywhere, anytime. Something big and disgusting that'll really freak the Cadwalladers out. And we need *lots* of them, a whole army of them if we can get it, in just a few days. Mum and Dad could easily find another buyer by the weekend. We don't have much time.'

I nodded. Hornets were great, but no war was ever won with an airforce alone. We needed ground troops.

An army of well-trained combat soldiers, to invade and conquer enemy territory.

It had to be a large insect, too. Invading the Cadwalladers with an army of trained fleas wouldn't do much good. But how many large insects were up to the job?

'Stick insects?' I said doubtfully. 'Grasshoppers? Dung beetles?'

'Forget it,' Emma said quickly. 'Not enough of them.'

'Aphids? Earwigs? Ladybirds?'

'Ladybirds!' Emma gasped in mock horror, and put a hand up to her mouth. 'No! I'm so scared!'

'Well, you come up with some then. You're the insect expert.'

'I'm trying, I'm trying. If you'd just let me *think*—'

Just then a cockroach scuttled out from under the bench. An enormous dark brown one with thick black stripes on its back. Without thinking I stomped on it. I felt the skeleton crunch underfoot, and the goo of its insides splat across the bottom of my shoe.

I froze.

I looked at Emma.

Emma looked at me.

I lifted up my foot and we gazed together at the gooey mess on the bottom of my shoe.

'That's it!' Emma exclaimed excitedly. 'Cockroaches!! Of course, they'd be perfect! They're big and disgusting. People are scared of them. They can go anywhere. And there are *millions* of them! I've got a formula for catching cockroaches, too, just like I use with the hornets. Come on, I'll show you. We'll get started right now.'

We were both so eager to get going, we could hardly contain ourselves. For so long we'd been so miserable and felt so helpless, we'd almost forgotten what it felt like to have hope. It was wonderful. Sure, there was still a long way to go—we both knew that. There were a lot of problems to be solved in a very short space of time.

But the point was, there was light at the end of the tunnel now.

We could see it. Both of us could.

That same night, working only in our garage, we caught twenty cockroaches. Emma's formula worked a treat. It wasn't Princess Pixie bubble bath this time. It was raspberry cordial concentrate mixed with bicarbonate of soda. And it wasn't in a bucket—it was in a big clear-plastic fishbowl.

Emma got the fishbowl out of the cupboard next to the bench. She set it down in the middle of the garage floor, in front of the car, and sprinkled a thick layer of bicarb on the bottom. Using the electric kettle from the kitchen, she boiled up half a litre of water, added quarter of a cup of raspberry cordial, and poured the steaming cherry-red mixture in on top of the bicarb in a single glugging rush.

The reaction was instantaneous. The bicarb erupted in a fizzing, frothing, shimmering red mass of bubbles. Not big bubbles, like the bubbles made by the Princess Pixie, but tiny, high-energy bubbles, dancing and glimmering madly inside the bowl.

'Quick!' Emma shouted, as soon as she'd finished pouring. 'Get up on the bench, out of the way!'

She made a run for it with the kettle. I dashed after her, and in two seconds flat we were crouched together up on the bench, looking down.

At exactly the moment we stopped moving, the first cockroach came out of the woodwork.

It scuttled up to the outside of the fishbowl, then stopped. It waved its antennae at the bubbles fizzing and frothing on the other side of the see-through plastic. Another cockroach joined it. Then another. In less than a minute a dozen of the loathsome creatures were gathered together, entranced by the strange and beautiful display inside the bowl.

'Can they see it?' I whispered to Emma. 'Or can they hear it? What makes them come?'

'They can *feel* it,' Emma whispered gleefully. 'They can feel the minute vibrations of the bubbles. It's like delicate music to them. They can't resist it. And they can smell the raspberry cordial, too, which is absolutely their favourite food. Watch what happens next.'

The fizzing sound was beginning to die out, but that didn't deter the cockroaches. One of them had started climbing up the outside of the bowl. As if inspired, the others joined it, and in a very short space of time they had all climbed to the top and dropped down over the rim to feast on the red cordial mix at the bottom.

'And now they're trapped,' Emma said with a smile. 'They can climb in, but they can't get out again. See?'

I watched, fascinated, as more cockroaches came scuttling out of the woodwork. The newcomers climbed up the fishbowl and dived in, just as the first group had done.

'Won't the bicarb hurt them?' I asked.

'No. It's not poisonous. And even if it was, cockroaches are super tough. The only way to kill them for sure is to stomp on them—squish them—like you did earlier. But we're not trying to kill these babies. These are going to be founding members of our first battalion.'

Emma got down from the bench and picked up her cordless drill. She tested it quickly to see if the batteries were still working, then strolled over to the fishbowl and calmly picked out a cockroach from inside.

'*Blattella germanica*,' she said in a formal, scientific voice. 'A German cockroach. They're the small ones with the stripes. The larger ones with no stripes are *Periplaneta americana*, the American cockroach. They've both got the same life span, the same mating habits. They eat the same food. There's not much to choose between them, really, except in size.'

I got down and joined her. The bubbling inside the fishbowl had ceased. All the cockroaches were feasting royally on the bicarb and raspberry cordial. As far as I could tell, only two American cockroaches were present. I liked them at first because they were bigger, but after observing them for a while I noticed they were slower than the German cockroaches, and sort of dull-looking. I know that's a funny thing to say about cockroaches, but the German cockroaches looked shiny and tough and battle-hardened, ready for immediate action.

'Stormtroopers and US Marines,' I said. 'Both in the same army. Wow.'

I was interrupted by the sound of Emma drilling expertly into the first cockroach's head.

It took us five minutes to equip all twenty cockroaches with microchip radio receivers, and then apply superglue over the holes. We used one of Emma's plastic buckets to store the cockroaches in when we'd finished with them. Emma found a lid which wedged down tightly all round the rim, and made sure they couldn't get out.

I was itching to see if we could steer them the way we'd steered the hornet, but Emma made me wait till they were all done.

'We've got to be able to move them together, with one handset,' Emma said. 'We should be able to, if all their receivers are set to the same frequency. In theory we should be able to set one battalion at one frequency, and another battalion at a different frequency, so each battalion can be controlled by a different handset. It'll get tricky once we get more than four battalions, though, because we've only got two hands each.'

'How many in each battalion?' I asked.

'A thousand,' Emma answered. 'That's big enough to successfully attack a human being. But it's not *too* big. I'm thinking we should have two battalions in a regiment, so we can comfortably control one regiment each.'

I nodded. 'I want a regiment of Germans,' I said, after a pause. 'Those Americans look slack.'

Emma turned and gave me a cold military stare.

'I'm the Commander-in-Chief here, buster,' she said. 'You'll get what you're given.'

She took the lid off the bucket and gently shook the eighteen German cockroaches onto the floor. She kept the two American cockroaches trapped inside, for later.

As soon as the cockroaches hit the ground they began to scatter. I began to run after them, thinking they were getting away, but Emma shouted at me to stop. She scooped up the handset from the bench and switched it on. Immediately all of the cockroaches froze.

'How'd you do that?' I asked.

'It's the transmitter inside the microchip,' Emma explained. 'Even though I'm not using the trigger, it's sending out a low-grade signal. It's the same sort of signal the nerve centre gives out when it tells the body to stop moving.'

Next, Emma performed a very strange manoeuvre with her handset. She pulled the trigger in hard, making the cockroaches go full speed ahead. At the same moment she jerked the handset hard upwards in front of her, as if pulling sharply on a fishing line.

The cockroaches, all at the same time, leapt a metre into the air. Straight up and down— *kaboing!!!*—like fleas in a flea circus. One jumped up right in front of me, and just missed hitting me on the nose.

As soon as they jumped Emma switched her handset off. When they landed, they all rushed together to form a huddle in front of the car.

Emma switched her handset back on again and they froze.

'Why did they just run in like that?' I asked. 'What happened?'

'Self-defence,' Emma explained. 'It's an instinctive reaction when I make them jump. They know they can't get away, so they band together for protection. I've done it before with different kinds of beetles but that's the first time I've tried it with cockroaches.'

I gazed at the tight formation of cockroaches in delight. 'Excellent!' I said. 'So all you have to do is hit the juice and jerk the handset up, and they'll all come rushing in together?'

Emma nodded. 'Every time.'

For the next hour we put the cockroaches through their paces. Emma marched them in circles around the car. I practised the jumping manoeuvre with them, over and over again, until I got it exactly right. Emma marched them up the side of her cupboard onto the bench. I marched them straight up the brick wall and across the ceiling. We did speed trials from the front of the garage to the back. We put blocks of wood down on the floor and practised manoeuvring the cockroaches in around them.

When we'd had enough, Emma drove the cockroaches back up the side of the bucket and over the rim. We put the lid on and switched the handset off, then we did a couple of high-fives. I danced around in front of the bench shouting, *'Boom boom boom, I'll take you to my room! Go-o-o-o-o cockroaches!'*

'We're going to get you, Dick Cadwallader!' Emma shouted.

'You too Shaun and Ian!' I echoed.

'See how you like it when you have to sell YOUR house!'

'See how you like it when YOU can't sleep at night!'

'When you've got cockroaches crawling all over you!'

'In your mouth and up your bum!'

'You better watch out! The cockroaches are coming! Woooo-HOOOOOO!'

12

the great bucket disaster

Our first and most serious problem was numbers. We had twenty cockroaches so far. We needed thousands.

And we needed them caught, equipped and trained within a few days.

After breakfast the following morning Emma told me we were taking a bus into town. She told Mum we were going to the movies, but she wouldn't say where we were *really* going until we were standing at the bus stop, holding two plastic buckets and a fishbowl, as well as bucket lids, two bottles of raspberry cordial concentrate, four large packets of bicarb and an electric kettle.

'We're going to the paper warehouse at Dad's work,' Emma said to me. 'In the basement of the *Mirror Sun* building in town. Don't you remember Dad took us there last year, and we saw all those cockroaches behind the paper reels?'

I nodded. Dad had taken us to meet the storeman, a crusty old Scotsman named Dave. We'd had a ride on the forklift and Dave had shown us how the fork-lift lifted a reel, which was when we'd seen the cockroaches.

'There were only about fifty of them, but,' I said. 'Or maybe a hundred, max.'

'A hundred behind *one reel*,' Emma corrected me. 'And how many reels were there?'

'Heaps,' I admitted.

'I'm guessing the whole place is crawling with them,' Emma went on. 'A big old building like that just has to be.'

'So we catch them and carry them home in the buckets?' I asked. 'Is that the plan?'

Emma nodded. 'We can leave the rest of the stuff at the warehouse, for when we go back to get more. The only thing I haven't figured out yet is how to get inside.'

'You don't know how to get in?'

'Not without the storeman seeing us. If he did he'd tell Dad, which would be a disaster after what happened with the hornet. Dad'd just think we were trying to sabotage another sale.'

We got off outside the *Mirror Sun* building, and stood for a while in the carpark, getting our bearings. The *Mirror Sun* building was twenty storeys high, made entirely of concrete and steel. Combined with the carpark it took up a whole city block.

'There's a loading bay for trucks around the back,

I remember,' Emma told me. 'Where they deliver the paper. Maybe we can sneak in there.'

We walked behind the building and eventually found the loading bay. It was deserted. Emma and I had no trouble sneaking inside the open roll-a-door and creeping along the wall.

'Where to now?' I whispered.

'Anywhere, I guess,' Emma answered. 'Somewhere where no one can see us.'

We came to a dark corner. We were almost completely surrounded by massive shelves stacked up with huge reels of paper. Emma set the fishbowl down on the floor and began to get ready. Suddenly she put her hands to her mouth in alarm.

'The kettle!' she said. 'How stupid of me! I need somewhere to plug it in!'

'You need some water too,' I said. 'Here, give it to me, I'll go look for a tap.'

I took the kettle and ran back outside. I found a tap not far from the entrance to the loading bay, next to an industrial drain. By the time I'd filled the kettle and run back in, Emma had found a power point just inside the roll-a-door.

Three minutes later we had boiled water.

Five minutes later we had a spectacular display of cherry-red bicarb bubbles fizzing and frothing inside the fishbowl.

Six minutes later we were under siege. We were swamped by a flood of cockroaches.

They came from everywhere. From all directions at once. They came out from behind the paper and under the shelves. They came down from cracks in the ceiling and poked through holes in the skirting boards.

Hundreds of them. Maybe as many as five hundred, half a battalion, all at once. The noise they made was dry and rustly and utterly disgusting. It sent a chill running up my spine.

They scuttled to the bottom of the fishbowl with their antennae waving, and pushed up against it, like a crowd at a rock concert pressing towards the stage.

They began to climb.

Emma and I watched, fascinated and horrified, as the bowl disappeared under a seething carpet of brown. Fifty at a time the cockroaches clambered up the outside of the plastic and dived headlong over the rim.

In less than a minute the bowl was full. Excited cockroaches were trampling on each other, burrowing down through a mass of glistening bodies, trying to get one last bubbly taste of raspberry cordial before it all disappeared.

More cockroaches were coming. Another two or three hundred were milling around the bowl. We needed to empty it now and reset the trap, but how could we get past all those cockroaches? They were still hypnotised by the fizzing of the bubbles, even though the sound had almost died out. I didn't think they'd scatter out of our way.

'Do I do it or do you?' Emma asked.

'You're the Commander-in-Chief,' I said.

'As your Commander-in-Chief, I order *you* to do it.'

'No way. Sorry, but I'll spew if I go out there.'

Emma picked up a bucket. She glared at me in disgust.

'Coward,' she muttered. 'I'll see you court-martialled for this.'

'Yeah, if those cockroaches don't eat you first.'

She set out, walking slowly across the seething carpet of cockroaches that surrounded the bowl. Some of the cockroaches scattered out of her way, but most didn't. She trod on half a dozen with every step. The wet, squishing, crunching sound under her shoes, every time she moved forward, was sickening.

But not as sickening as the way they swarmed all over her legs when she stopped to pick up the bowl.

She had to grab the bowl by the rim to tip it into the plastic bucket. As soon as she did this, the cock-roaches panicked. Suddenly they didn't care about the bubbles anymore. They raced up Emma's arms, jumped onto her shorts and T-shirt, and ran helter-skelter down her bare legs.

I would've yelled my lungs out if it'd been me, but Emma didn't. Somehow she managed to lift that bowl right up, tip its load of cockroaches into the plastic bucket, then wedge the lid down tight, all without making a sound.

Finally, when she'd finished, she stood calmly brushing off the remaining cockroaches with her hands.

I decided right then and there that Emma *deserved* to be Commander-in-Chief. But I couldn't resist ribbing her a little when she got back.

'Well done!' I said. 'Great job! Ever thought of being a cockroach farmer?'

'Shut your mouth,' Emma growled. 'My *God* that was disgusting! You have no *idea*—!'

'You missed a couple. I think they went up your pants.'

She swung a fist at me. I ducked and ran off. 'All in the name of science, right?' I called back, as she chased me through the warehouse towards the door.

Emma calmed down soon enough. I went to get more water from the tap outside, and we repeated the process again.

After we'd repeated it four times, we had a bucketful.

After we'd repeated it sixteen times, we had four bucketsful, and we were ready to go home.

We'd been in the warehouse for more than three hours. Emma had got so used to having cockroaches swarming over her, she hardly noticed them anymore. When she came back the last time, after emptying the bowl into the bucket, I had to tell her that she had five of them crawling in her hair.

Then, in the bus on the way home, came the Great Spilled Bucket Disaster.

You can probably guess what happened. We lugged our four buckets back to the bus stop, loaded down with cockroaches, and waited for the bus. One of my buckets had a lid that didn't quite fit properly. It kept lifting loose. I wedged it down twice, then left it for a while, and when no cockroaches escaped, I forgot all about it.

When the bus arrived we hoisted our buckets up the steps. The buckets were pretty heavy—about the same weight as a schoolbag loaded down with books.

If you listened very carefully, with your ear right down to the lid, you could *hear* the cockroaches, rustling and scraping inside.

Fortunately nobody on the bus was listening that closely.

Halfway along Dagenham Road, the trouble began. I happened to look down at the buckets beside me on the floor. What I saw made my heart leap right into my mouth.

The loose lid had lifted up again. It was almost off.

Six sets of cockroach antennae were poking out from underneath.

No cockroach bodies yet. Just antennae. But if the bus hit a pothole, or if we got stuck at the lights with the engine idling, that lid would come right off.

I didn't say anything to Emma. It was my problem—I would fix it by myself. All I had to do was lean forward and jam the lid down hard, so it wedged tight again. Those six unfortunate cockroaches at the top would have their antennae chopped off, but all the others would be safely trapped inside.

I leant forward and put both hands on the rim. I pushed downwards with all my strength. At that exact same moment the bus driver hit the brakes hard, the bucket spun sideways on the slippery floor and tipped over, and I lurched, stomach first, into a sudden frenzied avalanche of brown insects swarming all over me.

I leapt to my feet with cockroaches in my hair and in my face, on my arms and under my clothes. I hollered blue murder. Everyone else on the bus hollered blue murder too. The cockroaches were up on the seats, scuttling into shopping bags, running up ladies' dresses and down men's shirts. It was chaos.

The driver swerved immediately to the side of the road. He opened the bus doors and everyone fled down the steps onto the footpath. They stood swatting cockroaches off themselves, shrieking and howling.

The driver and the other passengers were so furious with us, they made us get off the bus and walk.

When we got home with the remaining three buckets, Emma ordered me straight into the garage. She made me stand at attention in front of the bench, and gave me a proper army-style dressing down.

'First rule of a good military operation!' she shouted at me. 'Check your equipment! Report any faults immediately! Faulty equipment means the operation fails! Good men die! You understand that, soldier?'

'Sorry, Em.' I mumbled. 'I just slipped, I—'

'Yes sir, Commander sir!' Emma corrected me.

'Don't call me Em! It's time you lower ranks started showing me some RESPECT!'

'Yes sir, Commander sir,' I repeated. 'But what rank am I exactly, Commander sir? We haven't—'

'Q-U-I-E-T!!!' Emma stomped her foot furiously. 'Who asked you to speak? Nobody! Your stupidity just cost us a whole regiment! If we didn't have an attack planned for the next few days, I'd have you in solitary confinement for a month! I'd have you EATING cockroaches! All the ones you so kindly helped to escape! I'd have you scrubbing floors and peeling potatoes with the cadets back at the academy, you pathetic, snivelling, good-for-nothing worm! DO YOU UNDERSTAND???!!!'

I cringed and stared at the floor guiltily. I felt terrible. This was much worse than getting an earbashing from Dad.

'Yes sir, Commander sir,' I mumbled hoarsely.

'The future of 388 St Clairs Road, Dagenham depends on you, soldier,' Emma went on grimly. 'Never forget that. Never. Now drop and give me fifty.'

'Fifty what?' I asked.

'FIFTY PUSH-UPS, YOU MISERABLE PUS-FILLED BOIL ON A RAT'S BOTTOM!' Emma roared. 'AND MAKE IT SNAPPY! I HAVEN'T GOT ALL DAY!'

13

getting ready

We made two more trips to the warehouse. Then we began the long, laborious task of inserting microchips into all the cockroaches' heads.

If you've ever worked on a factory assembly line, or watched someone else work on one, you'll have a fair idea what it was like. Pick up a cockroach and hold it. Drill a hole in its head. Stick in a microchip, and fill up the hole with superglue. Chuck it in a bucket marked 'GERMAN' or a bucket marked 'AMERICAN', taking care not to let any of the other cockroaches escape. Then pick up another cockroach from one of the unmarked buckets, and repeat the whole thing over again.

We worked till nine o'clock on Tuesday night and fell into bed exhausted. We got up at dawn the following morning and started again.

By 10.30 Wednesday we'd finished the lot—six

thousand, three hundred and twelve cockroaches in total.

We had two battalions of a thousand American cockroaches and four battalions of a thousand German cockroaches. The two American cockroach battalions combined to form one regiment. The four German cockroach battalions combined to form another two regiments. The three hundred and twelve leftovers (mostly Americans) were put into reserve, in case we suffered casualties or we wanted to enlarge the army later on.

We stored the cockroaches by the battalion. One battalion per bucket. A thousand cockroaches could fit inside one bucket easily, with plenty of room to move and air to breathe.

Just to be on the safe side, Emma drilled small holes in the side of each bucket. She also drilled a slightly larger hole in the top so we could squirt in raspberry cordial concentrate.

We labelled each bucket clearly with the name of the battalion inside. For example, one bucket was labelled 2ND BATTALION, 2ND GERMAN REGIMENT. Another was labelled 1ST BATTALION, 2ND AMERICAN REGIMENT.

After that was done I passed each bucket in through Emma's bedroom window and she stacked them up in her wardrobe.

Then we sat down to eat lunch and discuss tactics.

Emma wanted to launch our first attack that same evening, while Dick Cadwallader hosted his regular Wednesday night gambling party. She wanted to send our six new cockroach battalions in an all-out assault, to see what damage they could do.

'It all depends on how well we can manoeuvre them,' she explained to me as we ate our sandwiches in her bedroom. 'Listen carefully. I'll tell you how it works. Each of the six battalions has its own radio-frequency and its own handset, as we discussed earlier. But each battalion also has a *regiment* frequency and its own *regiment* handset, so you can move two battalions at once. If you want to change from one to the other you simply switch on the regiment handset, which over-rides the battalion one. Switch off the regiment handset, and the cockroaches revert to battalion frequency. You got that?'

'I think so,' I nodded. 'I mean, yes sir, Commander sir. Affirmative. So the maximum each of us can control at one time is two regiments? One regiment handset in each hand?'

'Correct. There may be times when we need to attack in battalions, and other times when we need to attack in regiments. I don't know yet. I'm viewing tonight as pretty much a trial run, to sort all this out.'

'What if we want to leave one battalion or regiment where they are for a while?' I asked. 'And concentrate on attacking with another one?'

'You just leave the handset in neutral,' Emma said.

'Remember? When you do that while the handset is still on, the cockroaches freeze. But don't leave them anywhere too exposed or they'll be vulnerable to counter-attack. Be sure to scout out the battlefield for cover.'

I thought over what Emma had said. It seemed like she'd covered all the angles.

All of a sudden a problem hit me. 'But Em—' I began. 'I mean, excuse me, Commander sir, how are we going to scout out the battlefield? We'll be hiding out of sight with our handsets, won't we?'

Emma nodded. 'That's correct, soldier. We'll be headquartered in the command-and-control centre, which is here.'

'Here?' I repeated, staring at her blankly. 'You mean right here in your bedroom?'

'Correct.'

'But—but if we're here in your bedroom, how are we going to be able to see anything at all? The cockroaches'll be over the wall inside the Cadwalladers' place!'

A slow smile spread across Emma's face. 'I was wondering when you'd get to that,' she said. 'Why don't you take a look under my bed, and bring out what you find there. That might help you answer your question.'

I went to Emma's bed and lifted up the bedspread. Peering underneath, I caught sight of a very strange piece of equipment indeed. It resembled an enormous computer keyboard with two small television screens set into it. Beneath each screen was a complicated set of buttons and switches and knobs. Next to it was a long length of coiled black cable attached to an antenna.

I dragged both items carefully out into the middle of the floor, and looked at them in amazement.

'What's all this?' I asked.

'A portable dual-screen multiband ultra-high-frequency amplifier-receiver,' Emma explained. 'The receiver is specially designed for picking up weak close-range UHF signals. I spent years saving up for it, and for the cameras that go with it. It was all part of my experiments with butterflies. I never thought I'd be using it in a war.'

Her face clouded over for a moment. I got up and sat next to her on the bed.

'So where are the cameras?' I asked.

Solemnly, Emma pointed at the collection of five tall glass jars grouped together on her desk. Propped up inside each jar was a twig. Perched on each twig was a butterfly. The butterflies were all quite large, and extremely beautiful. One was plain yellow, one was blue, one was bright orange, one was multi-coloured, and one was a mixture of dark brown and black.

I was used to Emma's butterflies. They didn't impress me as much as they used to. Especially not when I was supposed to be looking for cameras.

'Where?' I repeated. 'I still can't see them.'

'Look closer,' Emma advised.

I got up and went over to her desk. I couldn't see any cameras anywhere. I was searching for something big and bulky with a handle and a zoom-lens.

But there was nothing big and bulky on Emma's desk.

There were only five glass jars with a single, delicate-winged butterfly inside each—

I couldn't believe it when I finally saw the cameras. They were *tiny*. They were approximately the same size as a grain of cooked white rice. Each one was strapped around a butterfly's neck by a hair-thin silver wire.

'Those are *cameras?*' I said in a hushed, incredulous voice. 'They take *pictures?*'

'Very good pictures, actually,' Emma replied. 'High-resolution. Good quality colour. I've only got five of them, but five cameras should give us a good enough view if we position them right.'

'But how are we going to do that?' I asked.

'How d'you think? The same way we position the cockroaches. And the same way we'd position the hornets, if we had any.'

'Microchips!' I grinned wildly. 'You've put micro-chips in their heads! So we can steer them!'

'Exactly.' Emma got up off the bed to join me. 'These are remote-controlled butterflies. Strictly for reconnaissance, they wouldn't be much good in a fight. Butterflies aren't exactly vicious predators, like hornets. They're not disgusting enough to scare anybody, either, like cockroaches. But they're very important to our plan. We go in first with these, position them exactly where we want them, then freeze them for the duration of the battle. Then we use the pictures they send back to guide our glorious cockroaches to victory.'

'Wicked,' I breathed. 'That's totally wicked, Em— I mean sir, Commander sir.'

Emma looked at her watch.

'In fact, I think we need to start sending them in right now,' she said. 'The rest of the army can enjoy some R&R, but these butterflies have work to do. Their handsets are stacked in the top drawer. Take them out and get them ready will you, soldier? Operation Party Pooper is about to get under way.'

14

operation party pooper

At 2.28 that Wednesday afternoon our first two remote-controlled butterflies were let loose from Emma's bedroom.

I was flying one of the butterflies. Emma was flying the other. Emma had plugged in her portable dual-screen multiband ultra-high-frequency amplifier-receiver, which she called a PDSM for short.

It had taken nearly half an hour to set everything up properly. Emma had ordered me to climb up the drainpipe and position the antenna on the roof, so we could get a good signal from the Cadwalladers' place, once the butterflies had gone.

When that was done she'd set the frequencies on the PDSM's channels to match the frequencies being transmitted by the butterflies.

'At any one time we can get pictures from two of the five butterfly-cams,' she said. 'Any of the five can come up on any of the two screens. The switches change the camera, the knobs fine-tune the reception, and the buttons zoom in for a close-up or pan out to a wide shot. That clear?'

'Affirmative.'

'Good. This is where you prove what you're made of, soldier. Are you made of the right stuff?'

'Yes sir, Commander sir!'

'Then let's go.'

Now our butterflies were fluttering high over Dick Cadwallader's security fence, heading into his front courtyard. Emma and I were seated in front of the PDSM, hunched forward holding our handsets, staring intently at the images flickering on the screens.

'It's jiggling, it's jiggling everywhere!' I shouted. 'I can't see a thing!'

'Head for the balcony above the front door!' Emma shouted back. 'I'm going for the corner of the garage! Hold on, we're closing in fast!'

It was ten times harder than steering the hornet. And a hundred times harder than steering the cockroaches. Every time the butterfly flapped its wings, the camera mounted on its neck jerked and jiggled like it was strapped to a wild bucking bronco.

It was like trying to land a plane in the middle of a cyclone, while the airport below was being torn apart by an earthquake. It was damn near impossible.

Three times I approached the balcony. Three times

I had to abort the landing and veer away, just as I was about to hit the wall.

'Do you have touchdown yet?' Emma asked after the second time.

'Negative, Commander! That's a negative!'

'I'm at the garage, I'm at the garage!' Emma said excitedly. 'I have touchdown! Everything's looking good! Securing Camera One's position—NOW!'

She took her finger off the trigger and waited a moment. She put her handset down triumphantly on the desk and grinned at me.

I didn't grin back. My own butterfly was totally out of control.

The third time I'd veered away, I'd jammed my finger hard on the trigger to get up airspeed. The butterfly couldn't cope with that much power. Its wings got tangled up with each other. It began spiralling dizzily down towards the ground.

'I'm losing altitude, I'm losing altitude! Mayday! Mayday-y-y!'

The butterfly hit the garden around the back of the Cadwalladers' swimming pool with a soft bump. The picture on the screen went fuzzy for a second. Then it cleared.

I touched the trigger gently and nudged the handset upwards. To my great delight, the butterfly took to the air.

'We're up again! Damage minimal! All systems are go!'

'Here, give me that.' Emma reached for my hand-set. 'You're going to kill it if you keep this up.'

'No, I won't! I'll land it properly this time, I promise!'

The trick, I'd just realised, was to come in slowly. Very, very slowly. Butterflies don't like going fast.

I relaxed, and let the butterfly go at its own speed.

My finger was only barely touching the trigger. Now the jiggling was in slow motion, and I could see the Cadwalladers' house a lot better on the screen.

I aimed for the edge of the balcony and got it, first time. Perfect.

I took my finger off the trigger and turned the butterfly in a smooth arc, three hundred and sixty degrees.

'Camera Two in position, Commander!' I said. 'No sweat!'

'Well done, soldier. Good flying.'

'What now? Do we bring in the next two butter-flies?'

'Not just yet. Let's have a look around. We haven't seen inside the Cadwalladers' fence since they built the new house.'

We studied the pictures on the two screens. The first thing I noticed was how crowded the Cadwalladers' new frontyard was. The house was jammed up against the garage. The garage was jammed up against the deck. The deck was jammed up against the pool and the pool was jammed up against the security fence, where it bordered our house.

'Check out inside, through the double doors under the balcony,' Emma said. 'Dick's in there talking to someone. I'm sending in Camera One.'

I peered closer. Sure enough, Dick Cadwallader was standing in a big room beside a long dinner table, in front of a well-stocked bar. He was talking to his butler, the man I'd seen the day Dad punched Dick Cadwallader on the nose.

Emma picked up her handset and guided her butterfly expertly in through the double doors. The butterfly fluttered gently above Dick's head to the top shelf of the bar, and came to rest on a whisky bottle.

'Now we turn the audio on,' she said, 'so we can hear what they're saying.'

Emma flicked a switch on the PDSM and twiddled with a knob. There was a short burst of static, then I heard Dick's voice, loud and clear.

'What d'you think this is, a McDonald's?' Dick was saying. 'A Black Stump Steakhouse? The frogs' legs come out *after* the monkeys' brains, you halfwit! If you bring the frogs' legs out first, then no one can taste the brains properly because they're ruined by the squid's ink you dip the frogs' legs into! Any fool knows that! And for Pete's sake don't bring the caviar out before the mountain oysters, or the whole place'll be in chaos! I've got a reputation to uphold, y'know! I can't have this sort of garbage going on!'

The butler apologised abjectly. I turned to Emma and whispered, 'What are mountain oysters?'

'Goats' testicles,' Emma replied. 'They're great, you should try them. Soft and smooth on the outside, lumpy in the middle.'

'Now go and tell Chef he's made a mistake, and tell him I'll give him a good clout round the ear next time I see him!' Dick went on. 'Then you can go upstairs to my study and print out a hundred new menus, with all the food in the proper order this time! And I'll tell you what, if you stuff this up again on Saturday, when I've got all my sponsors and financial advisers coming, I'll have your guts for garters! It's going to be the biggest evening of my life, that party! It's when I say thank you to everyone who's helped me become the successful, dynamic, forward-thinking businessman that I am today. You bring the frogs' legs out before the monkeys' brains, boy-o, and it'll be *your* brains I serve up, beaten nice and tender with a sledgehammer! You got me?'

The butler apologised a second time and hurried off. Dick strode across to the bar and poured himself a stiff drink. He downed it in a single gulp, muttered something about how hard it was to get good help these days, then disappeared up a nearby staircase.

Emma turned to me and smiled impishly.

'Sounds to me like Dick's under a bit of pressure,' she said. 'And he's got a big party coming up this Saturday, too. I think we might've got our cockroaches ready just in time.'

She picked up her handset and steered her butterfly up the stairs after Dick. We followed him down a long hall and up another flight of stairs, till he came to a heavy wooden door. He knocked on the door, then entered. Emma's butterfly fluttered in behind him and perched high up on some bookshelves.

'Ahhhhhh-h-h-h-!'

I couldn't help screaming at what I saw on the screen. I dived for the floor with my hands clamped tightly over my eyes. Emma screamed too, and tumbled backwards over her chair, so she ended up on the floor right beside me.

It was horrible.

It was the most grotesque, repulsive thing I'd ever seen.

The nurse was in the room with Beverly Cadwallader, changing her nappy.

The nurse was using a thick rope threaded through a pulley on the ceiling and attached to a winch. She was winching Beverly's bottom up off the floor. Beverly still had her old nappy on, but her huge, spongy, flabby, trunklike legs were dangling in mid-air, right in front of the camera.

The old nappy was wet, too. It had that saggy, yellow look that a nappy gets when it's full of wee. I'd seen a few fat babies with wet nappies in my life, but nothing—nothing remotely like this.

That nappy was so big, you could have wrapped a car up in it.

Not just a Holden Barina, either. A Commodore station wagon. Towing a trailer.

'*Ahhhh-h-h-h-h! Turn it off! Turn it off!*' I screamed.
'*It's awful, it's awful! Ahhhh-h-h-h-h!*'

Emma still had her handset. She staggered to her
feet and steered the butterfly safely out of the way.
I refused to get up off the floor until the nightmare was
over, and Beverly's nappy had been changed.

I finally got up just as Dick asked the nurse to leave
the room. Beverly was sitting up on a rug by this time,
playing with some wooden blocks, goo-ing and gaa-ing
happily.

Emma and I heard the door click shut as the nurse
went out.

Dick crouched down on the floor in front of
Beverly, and spoke to her softly.

'Bev? It's me, darl. It's Dick. I know you can't understand me, and you wouldn't recognise me from a
squashed cane toad, but I wouldn't mind a chat, if it's
all the same to you.'

He paused a moment, regarding his wife thoughtfully. Beverly blew a spit bubble and grinned at him.

'You know what I've bought so far this week,
darl?' he went on. ''Course you don't, you don't even
know what planet you're on, so I'll tell you. I've
bought another Aston Martin Spider, for a start. That
makes five of 'em. I've bought another helicopter—
that makes three of those and another boat as well,
which I need like a hole in the head, considering I
never have the time to go fishing. I spent twenty
thousand dollars buying top-of-the-line go-karts for

Shaun and Ian. I spent *thirty* thousand dollars flying baby turtles over from the Galapagos Islands, so Chef could make turtle soup for the party on Saturday night. I've spent a grand total of one million, seven hundred and sixteen thousand dollars in the first three days of this week, and I'll probably spend another million by Sunday night. And you know what? *I love it!* I love spending money! I love making money too, and we're doing plenty of that, don't worry. I love money more than anything else in the world, darl, except one thing. And that one thing is you.'

Dick shuffled forward and enveloped his wife in an awkward hug. She still had a wooden block in each hand, and began banging them playfully against the back of Dick's head. Dick didn't care.

'I'd give up every cent I had, if you could just be better again,' he said in a hoarse voice. 'If you could be the same woman you used to be—the light and centre of my life. I'd give it all up tomorrow if that could happen, but it's not going to, is it love? You're not going to get better. You're going to stay like this forever. So I might as well go right back down those stairs and start spending more money.'

He gave a deep, mournful sigh, and left the room. Emma guided her butterfly out after him in silence.

'Must be tough having a wife who wears nappies,' I said after a while. 'I almost feel sorry for him. Don't you?'

137

'Almost,' Emma agreed. 'But wait till tonight, when the music starts up and the helicopters start arriving. I don't think we'll feel too sorry for him then.'

15

a famous victory

By nine o'clock Dick's party was in full swing. The music was blasting. Helicopters were arriving on the roof at the rate of one every four and a half minutes.

Mum and Dad had gone to bed with blindfolds and earmuffs. They'd given us some too, and urged us to do the same. The blindfolds and earmuffs were very uncomfortable to wear because they were so bulky. They made our heads sweat and gave us splitting headaches in the morning. Neither Emma nor I had any intention of using them. Not that night, or ever again.

All five of our butterfly-cams were in place: two were positioned strategically around the deck and the pool, and one each on the helipad, the garage roof, and the gambling room, giving us an excellent view of everything that went on.

About eighty guests were present. Dress was very formal. The men were all in suits and bow ties. The women were in evening gowns. Most of the women were wearing (or should I say *dripping with*) glittering diamond jewellery around their necks and wrists.

Some gambling games—blackjack, roulette, poker—were set up on tables inside the room with the bar.

The food was outside. It was arranged on tables along the edge of the deck. Silver trays piled high with steaming monkeys' brains had been brought out. The guests were devouring them greedily, blowing on them first to cool them, then popping them into their mouths with their fingers and squishing them juicily between their teeth.

Cocktail waiters were dashing everywhere, serving drinks.

Food waiters were ferrying trays of monkeys' brains to the guests playing gambling games inside.

Lights from the helipad on the roof were criss-crossing the courtyard, bathing everything in a brilliant rainbow of colours.

Dick was playing poker at one of the gambling tables. His trademark red jacket was draped over the chair behind him. His shirtsleeves were rolled up and he was smoking an enormous cigar.

Our cockroaches were stacked up in their buckets under Emma's window. The handsets for each battalion and each regiment were labelled and laid out on the bed. The handsets for the butterflies were on Emma's desk, behind the PDSM, and there was one more handset at the front of Emma's desk.

This one was labelled DEATH SQUADRON, with a skull and crossbones drawn next to the words.

It was our secret weapon.

Emma had mixed up a bucket of Princess Pixie bubble bath in the middle of the afternoon. We'd got lucky and caught seven hornets in three hours. The hornets had all been equipped with microchips. We'd given them a quick test run. Now they were resting quietly in a glass jar next to the cockroaches.

The first combat phase of Operation Party Pooper was about to get under way.

Emma checked her watch. She nodded to me. I picked a handset up from the bed and opened her window.

'Prepare first battalion, first German regiment,' Emma commanded.

'Aye aye, sir.' I put the handset down on the window ledge, then hoisted the first bucket out the window, tipped it on its side, and got ready to remove the lid.

'Handset switched on?'

'Check.'

'Cockroaches in neutral mode?'

I opened the lid just a crack, and peered inside. None of the cockroaches were moving.

'Check.'

'Good luck, soldier,' Emma said. 'Proceed.'

I took the lid off and poured the thousand cockroaches into the garden. Their nerve centres were still jammed by the steady pulse of radio waves from the microchip. They lay exactly where they'd landed, as if dead.

I jump-started them, jamming my finger hard on the trigger for a split second and jerking the handset upwards. A thousand cockroaches leapt a metre into the air, then rushed together towards the edge of the driveway.

'Battalion in battle formation,' I reported.

'Prepare second battalion, first German regiment,' Emma said.

I did the same thing with the next bucket of cockroaches. I now had two thousand of them lined up in formation on the drive.

'Switch to regiment frequency and advance to attack-launch coordinates,' Emma ordered.

I left the two battalion handsets on the ledge and picked up a regiment handset. Peering out the window, I marched my regiment straight across the driveway, through the grass and under the trees on the other side, to the base of the Cadwalladers' security fence.

I left them in neutral and prepared the second German regiment, which I marched to exactly the same spot.

Emma now prepared her American regiment. She climbed out her window and marched them all the way down the drive to the Cadwalladers' front gate.

We were ready for our three-pronged attack.

Our battle plan centred on a diversion. Emma would send her American regiment in first, under the front gate and up the path. They would attack the food tables on the pool deck. While this was happening, my two German regiments would come over the wall and make a mad dash, along the front of the house, for the gambling room.

Here's an aerial map of the Cadwalladers' frontyard, to show you exactly where the cockroaches were coming in:

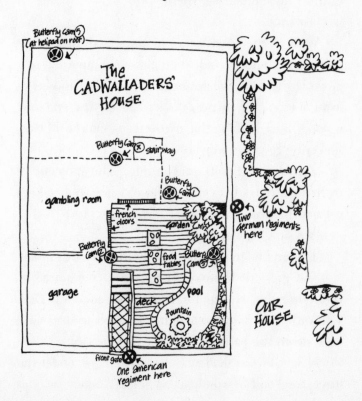

OPERATION PARTY POOPER

POSITION OF TROOPS AT COMMENCEMENT OF HOSTILITIES

Once inside the gambling room my aim was to drive everyone out onto the deck and cut them off from the stairway up to the helipad. As soon as all the guests were gathered outside, Emma would send in the Death Squadron.

The Death Squadron had three different assignments. The first was to sting as many guests as possible, out on the deck. The second was to patrol the helipad, and sting anyone trying to escape that way.

The third assignment was probably the most important. It was simple.

Get Dick.

With all the cockroaches in place, and the hornets still buzzing quietly inside their glass jar, Emma and I sat down at the desk. We arranged our various handsets in front of us, picked up the ones we needed first, and took a good, long look at the two screens on the PDSM, flickering gently in front of us.

'Zero hour,' Emma said grimly. 'The moment of truth has arrived. Let's give it all we've got, soldier. Let's get out there and kick some Cadwallader butt.'

'Yes sir, Commander sir!' I said.

'I'm sending in the Marines,' Emma advised. *'Now!'*

She pressed down on the trigger. We stared at the butterfly-cam mounted on the edge of Dick Cadwallader's balcony, looking across the deck and back down the path.

A dark brown shadow came sweeping in under the gate, like a gust of wind passing across a lake.

'Zoom in Camera One!' Emma called.

I hit the zoom button and the pool deck filled Emma's screen. About forty people were gathered on it, mostly up the far end in front of the food tables.

The monkeys' brains had been cleared away by this time. The tables now contained plates of crispy battered frogs' legs and bowls full of creamy black squids' ink dip.

Somebody screamed.

'Marines to battalion frequency!' Emma shouted. 'Stand by! I'm splitting them up!'

She snatched up two battalion handsets. The dark brown mass of cockroaches swarmed up onto the deck. One half of the cockroaches—the first American battalion—swarmed straight up the tablecloths and onto the plates of food. The other half—the second American battalion—kept right on going, attacking anyone or anything that stood in their path.

'Reinforcements!' Emma shouted. 'Send in the Stormtroopers! Now!'

She was losing control of her battalion on the ground. Cockroaches were scuttling up the legs of guests and crawling all over them, which was great. But the guests were running in all directions, and Emma had no control over where they went.

'Jump them!' I shouted. 'Jump them, before they break up!'

Emma jammed her finger on the trigger and switched the handset off. All over the deck, a thousand

American cockroaches leapt a metre high into the air, causing even more panic and more screaming than there had been before.

Emma's battalion surged together in the middle of the floor. She began steering them again. Meanwhile her other battalion was in full control of the food tables. They had covered the plates of frogs' legs and the bowls of squids' ink dip in a seething brown mass, and were now stationary. Emma had them in neutral.

Some of the guests were jumping into the swimming pool fully clothed.

'Stormtroopers over the wall!' I said. 'Heading for the gambling room!'

'Roger!' Emma called back. 'Watch out for feet! It's hell out there!'

I switched to Camera Two, which was perched on the roof of the garage above the deck, looking back towards our place. On it, I saw two full regiments of German cockroaches scuttling down the inside of the three-metre-high fence.

They hit the mulch behind the pool and kept going along the front wall of the house. I felt adrenalin pumping through my veins. Nobody had seen them yet. With a wild yell I steered them up onto the pool deck, near the front door and into the fray.

'I'm losing my second battalion!' Emma interrupted me suddenly. 'I can't hold them! They're going everywhere!'

'Jump them again!' I shouted back, but Emma only shook her head.

'It's no use! I'm letting them go! I'm bringing in the Death Squadron! You get everyone out from inside the house!'

I steered my two regiments in through the double doors and met heavy resistance. Everyone in the gambling room was rushing to get outside. Their shoes were trampling on cockroaches with every step. I switched to Camera Four, perched up on top of the bar, and split my two regiments up in the hope of lessening the carnage.

Then I jumped both regiments at once.

Four thousand cockroaches leapt into the air inside the gambling room. Pandemonium broke loose. Tables were upturned. Chairs fell over. Decks of cards, money and gambling chips flew everywhere.

In the corner of the screen I caught sight of Dick Cadwallader. He was desperately trying to calm people down. I knew Emma's Death Squadron would be arriving any minute. As soon as my regiments had regrouped, I steered them both straight at him to chase him outside.

He saw the cockroaches coming and started to run. He sprinted straight out the double doors then tripped and fell on the deck. No one else was left in the gambling room, so I parked one of my regiments there in neutral and steered the other one out after him.

I switched to Camera One again. Emma's second

battalion was nowhere in sight, and her first battalion was in serious trouble. It was still up on the food tables, parked there in neutral. Two waiters were advancing on it with cans of Baygon, spraying full bore.

'Emma, retreat, retreat!' I said. 'Where are you?'

'Camera Five, up on the roof!' Emma yelled. I glanced at her screen and saw that she was in command of the Death Squadron, attacking a group of three men and four women who were trying to get away in a helicopter.

'Bring them down!' I shouted. 'Save your battalion! Dick's out there too!'

I steered my regiment of German cockroaches towards the waiters holding the cans of Baygon, to draw their fire. Emma switched to Camera One and brought her battalion out of neutral. She hit reverse, and the cockroaches scuttled off the table, but not before some of them had been sprayed.

Two more waiters appeared with two more cans of Baygon. They began spraying at my regiment too. I retreated quickly, but I might still have suffered more casualties if the Death Squadron hadn't swooped out of the sky at exactly the right moment and stung the waiters on the face and arms.

'Way to go, Emma!' I yelled. 'Yeah! Sock it to 'em, babe!'

Emma cast me a furious, indignant glance.

'I mean, well done sir, Commander sir. Excellent flying.'

Emma was operating the Death Squadron and a

battalion of cockroaches both at the same time. Her skill was amazing. The battalion was swerving in and out of the crowd, herding them towards the front gate like a sheepdog herds sheep.

The seven hornets in full flight, buzzing at high speed around the heads of their intended victims, were terrifying.

Emma got Dick with them, just as she promised she would. All seven hornets came swooping out of the sky in a perfectly executed dive-bomb, and stung him repeatedly across the neck and shoulders.

He howled with pain and ran off with the last of his guests, down onto the path and out the front gate.

'They're on the run now soldier!' Emma called to me. 'I'll hold them at the gate. You scout around for any sign of my second battalion! They've got to be there somewhere!'

I parked my regiment in neutral and hit the zoom buttons on the PDSM to bring the deck into close-up.

The aftermath of the battle was a gruesome sight.

Squashed cockroaches were everywhere. Their bodies littered the courtyard from one side to the other. Some were only half-squashed. Some were still alive, their antennae waving feebly. Hundreds lay spinning on their backs, with their legs thrashing wildly in the air, dying from the effects of the Baygon.

There'd been no time to call up our reserves.

Not a single able-bodied survivor remained.

I brought Camera Two out of neutral and fluttered it gently down over the scene. Still no survivors appeared. With a lump in my throat, I picked up the second American battalion handset and squeezed the trigger gently. No response.

'Come in, second battalion,' I muttered, squeezing the trigger again. 'Come in, please, come in—'

'We've lost them, haven't we?' Emma said quietly. 'The whole battalion. Every last cockroach.'

'I got hit pretty bad too, Commander,' I said. 'Like you said, it was hell out there.'

Emma nodded slowly. Suddenly she looked completely exhausted. She turned to me and gave me a crooked, bleary-eyed smile.

'Bring Camera Two up to the gate,' she said. 'Let's have a look at this mob outside. That might cheer me up.'

I flew Camera Two to the front gate and perched it on top, facing the road. We looked eagerly at the picture on our screen.

We had won a famous victory. Every guest at Dick's party had been driven out onto the footpath—except for the seven up on the roof, who had been stung badly by the Death Squadron, but had got away.

All the guests were milling around in confusion. No one was talking. Many of the guests had hornet stings on their arms and shoulders, which they were nursing as best they could.

Some of the women had lost their jewellery. A few had lost shoes. Some of the men were talking on mobile phones, calling up taxis or helicopters to arrange a lift home.

Dick was sitting on the kerb with his head buried in his hands, all alone.

'Party's over, eh Commander?' I said cheerfully to Emma. 'We really kicked some Cadwallader butt!'

Emma kept staring at the picture on the screen.

'Yes, the operation was a great success,' she said quietly. 'But we've had heavy losses. We've got a lot of work to do before Saturday, when we launch our next attack. Let's bring the troops home.'

16

beggars can't be choosers

Our losses from Operation Party Pooper proved to be heavier than we thought.

Emma lost not only her entire second battalion, but half of her first battalion as well. I lost nearly a whole battalion of Germans in the final assault on the deck.

We sent out six thousand cockroaches. Only three and a half thousand came back.

The good news was that all seven hornets in the Death Squadron survived. They'd been fantastic. Without them, our losses would have been far greater, thanks to those waiters spraying the Baygon. We might never have driven the guests from the Cadwalladers' courtyard out onto the road.

We had plans to catch as many hornets as we could in the three days before Dick's next party.

First, however, we had to catch more cockroaches.

We were up at dawn the next morning, ready to take the first bus into town.

We made two trips that day, bringing home four bucketsful of cockroaches each time. Each bucketful contained roughly a thousand insects. Counting our reserves, that brought our numbers back up to nearly six regiments—three of Germans, three of Americans.

After lunch we began drilling holes in their heads and inserting microchips. We were getting pretty skilled at it now (our record was seven in one minute, and four hundred in an hour), but with eight thousand to get through, we knew it was going to be a long and tedious job.

The last thing we needed was interruption. Unfortunately, we were disturbed in the middle of the afternoon by Dick Cadwallader, who came over to talk to Mum about buying our house.

Emma saw Dick out on the footpath. She was having a break for a while, resting her eyes, which got sore after hours of precision drilling. I was in the garage, peeling bits of dried superglue off my hands, when she came running back in with an excited grin on her face.

'Come out, quick!' she said. 'Dick's outside! The pest exterminators have arrived!'

I went with her down the driveway. Four bright yellow vans were parked opposite the Cadwalladers. They looked exactly like the vans that came on Mondays to clean up after Dick's parties, but instead of SPICK'N'SPAN CLEANING SERVICES—NO MESS TOO LARGE, the sign on the side of the van now read: PESTCLEAR EXTERMINATION SERVICES—ONE FLASH AND THEY'RE ASH!

Dick was talking to a group of four men wearing gas masks and full-body protective suits. All of the men had spray-packs on their backs, filled with a glowing orange liquid. As we watched, the front gate opened and the nurse appeared, pushing Beverly Cadwallader in her wheelchair. Dick's butler came out next, followed by the blonde personal assistant in her skin-tight bodysuit.

The roll-a-door of Dick's three-car garage opened up. Shaun and Ian roared out, driving high-powered go-karts at breakneck speed.

'Hoi! You two!' Dick bellowed. *'Take it easy with those things, eh?'*

Shaun and Ian took no notice. They roared away up the footpath towards the end of the road, nearly killing a neighbour's cat.

With everybody out of the house, the exterminators got to work. They marched to Dick's front gate and got their spray nozzles ready. The man in front put a whistle to his mouth and blasted it piercingly. Then, in single file, they marched in through the gate, shouting in unison:

'Left! . . . Right! . . . Left! . . . Right! . . . Left!'

The gate shut behind them with a clunk.

There was another piercing blast on the whistle.

A minute later, a billowing orange gas cloud began rising above the three-metre concrete fence.

Dick applauded enthusiastically. He cupped his hands to his mouth and yelled to the exterminators inside—'*That's it, gas the lot of 'em! Murder the little beggars! Fill their lungs with poison! Melt their brains and burn their innards to a crisp! You little beauty-y-y-y-y!*'

The orange gas cloud rose higher and higher, until it enveloped the whole house. Dick gave a whoop, then put two fingers in his mouth and whistled loudly. He kept on applauding, nudging his butler and personal assistant who were standing beside him. They began applauding too.

Shaun and Ian came roaring back on their go-karts. They flew past Dick and the other three, and stopped in front of us with their engines idling.

'Hey look, Ian,' Shaun said, and pointed to me. 'More pests.'

'Yeah, these are really *big* ones,' Ian said.

'We'll have to get the exterminators over here when they've finished. Can't have bugs like *this* dirtying up the neighbourhood.'

Laughing and whooping, they swerved left and took off down our drive. They began doing doughnuts in front of our garage, revving their engines and leaving ugly black tyre marks on the concrete.

'Hey!' I shouted. 'You can't do that! Get off our drive!'

Emma and I ran to stop them. Shaun almost hit Emma in the back of the leg. I leapt on Ian and managed to drag him off his go-kart onto the grass.

'I said stop it! Get out of our driveway!'

'Get off me! Get off me, you little turd!'

He pushed me away and stood up. Shaun whizzed past just behind him and burnt some more rubber in front of the mailbox.

'You'll be sorry when our dad buys this place,' Ian said.

Emma joined me and stood with her arms folded. 'You don't know what you're talking about,' she said defiantly. 'My parents would never sell to *you*.'

'Wanna bet?' Ian smirked. 'They're pretty desperate, so we hear. And my dad's coming over right now to make your mum an offer she can't refuse.'

Sure enough, Dick Cadwallader appeared at the end of our drive. He strode to our front door without saying hello to the twins or to us. Mum was out the back hanging out some washing. It took her a while to answer the doorbell.

When she saw who'd come to visit, she wasn't too pleased.

'Hello, Dick,' she said coldly. 'What can I do for you?'

'G'day, Louise,' Dick replied. 'I was just passing, so I thought I'd drop by. I was wondering if you've been having problems with cockroaches lately. We had a plague of 'em last night at our place. Thousands of the little beggars. Ruined the little soirée I was having with a few friends. I've got the pest exterminators over at my place right now, and I thought maybe you might need 'em here too.'

Mum folded her arms and gave Dick Cadwallader a withering stare.

'If you're suggesting your cockroaches came from our place, think again,' Mum said. 'We've got no problem with cockroaches here.'

'Well, they have to be coming from somewhere, don't they?' Dick said. 'And let's face it, your house isn't exactly brand spanking new. It's old, it's run-down, kitchen cupboards are probably filthy—'

'My kitchen cupboards are *not* filthy,' Mum fumed. 'And if that's what ruined your party last night, I'm glad of it. I hope they plague you like you've been plaguing us. I hope they drive you stark raving mad.'

Dick looked uncomfortable for a moment, but forced himself to be calm.

'What're we arguing about this for, Louise?' he said. 'If you don't want the exterminators here, that's fine. I just thought it might help you sell the house, that's all. Nobody wants a place that's swarming with cockroaches, now do they?'

'It's not swarming with cockroaches and we don't need your help,' Mum said.

'Oh, you've had some offers, have you?' Dick raised his eyebrows in mock surprise. 'Now that's a shame, because I was going to make one. The kids're looking for somewhere to ride their new go-karts around, y'know, and they're not allowed on the road. I was thinking about bulldozing this place and putting a go-kart track here. What d'you reckon, kids?'

Shaun and Ian whooped enthusiastically.

'Might even have room for a mini-golf course down in the backyard, you never know.'

Shaun and Ian cheered some more.

'You're wasting your time,' Mum said, and started to close the door.

Dick thrust a foot into the doorway to hold it open.

'I'll give you exactly what you paid for it, Louise,' he said smugly. 'I can afford it, you know that. If I were you I'd have a word to Pat, see what he thinks. I've got a feeling he might think that's a pretty good offer. And you know what they say about people in your position, don't you, eh? Beggars can't be choosers, ha ha ha!'

That evening after dinner, Mum and Dad discussed Dick Cadwallader's offer. They asked us to leave them alone so they could talk. We went out to the garage and finished our work on the cockroaches for the day.

We'd conscripted three new battalions that day: two of Germans and one of Americans. Emma had also caught five more hornets, bringing the grand total in the Death Squadron to twelve.

Things were looking good for Saturday. As long as our parents didn't sell the house first.

'They won't sell to Dick Cadwallader,' I said

confidently to Emma. 'Not so he can bulldoze the house and put in a go-kart track. Not in a million years.'

Emma wasn't so sure. 'I don't think they've had many more offers,' she said. 'Maybe none at all.'

'Good!' I exclaimed. 'That means we've still got a chance to beat Dick with the cockroaches! After Saturday we have to attack him every day, I reckon. Every day and every night, until he can't stand living there any longer and he decides to sell.'

'Yes, that was my plan exactly,' Emma agreed. 'But it won't work if Mum and Dad sell first. If they *do* agree to take Dick's offer, I think we need to tell them about the cockroaches. Now. Tonight. That way, they might still think there's hope and give my plan a chance. Agreed?'

I thought this over carefully. I knew our parents were still mad at us—at me especially—after we'd scared away the buyers. And besides, they were both such honest, fair-minded, decent people, they might not agree that attacking Dick Cadwallader with cockroaches and hornets was a good idea.

On the other hand, if they decided to sell the house to Dick Cadwallader, and we did nothing, all was lost.

Our beautiful home would be bulldozed, replaced by a go-kart track and a mini-golf course for Shaun and Ian.

'Agreed,' I said.

We went back to the living room to see what our parents had decided. I knew as soon as I saw Mum that it wasn't good news.

She was very upset. She wasn't crying, but she looked extremely pale and tired. Dad looked worried, angry and determined all at the same time.

'You've decided to sell, haven't you?' Emma said.

'Emma, Toby, I want you both to listen,' Dad said quietly. 'What I have to say now isn't easy. Sometimes in life things don't go your way and you have to make difficult decisions. The decision your mother and I have made tonight—well, it's just about broken both our hearts. But the fact is, since our real estate agent got attacked the last time she came here, we've had no more interest in this place. Not a single phone call. Not a single inspection. Nothing.'

'You don't have to sell, Dad!' I burst in. 'You really don't! There's—'

'I'm afraid we do, mate.' Dad took my hand and squeezed it. 'We just have to swallow our pride and take what we can get. It hurts to have to sell to the Cadwalladers. I know that better than anybody. But it's a firm offer and we'd be mad to refuse it. We'll find another house just as good, I promise. With a park nearby and everything. Okay?'

Mum put her head in her hands and turned away. I looked at Emma in desperation. She stepped forward.

'Mum, Dad,' she said. 'Toby and I have something to show you. It's important—it might mean we don't have to sell the house. But it's kind of weird.'

'Emma invented an insect!' I burst in breathlessly. 'I mean, she invented a *remote-controlled* insect! We've got thousands of them! We attacked the Cadwalladers with them last night, and—'

'You *what?*' Mum said in horror.

'Shut up, Toby!' Emma hissed at me. 'Mum, please. Like I said, it's weird. It's not the way you or Dad would resolve the situation. But it really works. And all I'm asking is that you come and have a look right now and let me explain it before you decide to sell.'

Mum looked at Dad.

Dad shrugged.

'Looking can't hurt, can it?' he said.

So the four of us went together to Emma's bedroom.

17

a change of heart

Emma took the PDSM out from under her bed and set it up on her desk. I opened the boxes containing the handsets and set them out ready to be used.

I was about to open the wardrobe to get some cockroaches, when Emma shook her head.

'No, not those,' she said. 'The butterflies first. We need the cameras.'

Our parents stood off to one side, completely bewildered.

I released two butterflies out the bedroom window. Emma quickly gave me a handset. We sat down in front of the screens and began steering.

Two shaking, jiggling pictures of the Cadwalladers' security fence appeared in front of us.

'Is that the Cadwalladers' place?' Mum said. 'Good lord, it *is* the Cadwalladers' place! Emma, what is this? Are those butterflies giving you those pictures? What on earth is going on?'

'Can I explain later, Mum?' Emma said. 'Just watch for a while. It's going to be *very* entertaining.'

Dad was standing silent, directly behind me. I could feel his eyes watching me closely as I steered my butterfly high over the fence.

'Camera One in the courtyard!' I said. 'Watch out, the wind's up! It's blustery up here!'

'Camera Two approaching!' Emma said. 'Look for signs of movement! Let's see if we can find Dick!'

I flew to the top of one of the sun-umbrellas and perched there. I began swivelling my butterfly slowly around in a circle, scanning the terrain. Emma flew Camera Two into the room where the bar was, but came fluttering out again shortly afterwards.

'Nothing inside there,' she said. 'Turn your audio on. Maybe we'll hear something.'

I flicked my audio switch and straightaway heard a splash. I swivelled my butterfly sharply, so the camera focused on the pool.

Shaun and Ian were swimming by the fountain.

The water in the pool was a very strange colour. It sparkled eerily—almost metallically—with a million tiny bubbles.

'I've got the twins in the pool, but the pool's pink,' I said. 'It looks like someone dumped a ton of Princess Pixie bubble bath in there.'

I zoomed Camera One in closer and we all had a look. 'That's not Princess Pixie bubble bath,'

Dad said softly over my shoulder. 'That's pink champagne.'

No one said anything for a moment. Of course Dad was right. It *was* pink champagne. I should have recognised it sooner. I zoomed Camera One in closer still and we could see bubbles rising up to the surface and popping, exactly as they did in a glass.

'Good lord, Patrick,' Mum breathed. 'That's incredible. How big is that pool d'you think?'

'Sixty thousand litres,' Dad murmured, shaking his head. 'Maybe seventy. I've said this before, but I'll say it again. The man's mad.'

Emma perched Camera Two on the garage roof, facing the pool. I took Camera One right up to the house roof, three storeys above us, to give us a bird's-eye view.

'It's time to give Shaun and Ian a nice little surprise,' Emma said. 'Get some Marines for me, Toby. The entire first regiment. Two battalions ought to do the trick this evening.'

'Aye aye, Commander!' I said.

Dad tugged at my shirt as I walked to Emma's wardrobe.

'What's with this Commander business, squirt?' he said jokingly. 'You never call *me* Commander.'

'That's because you don't command an army,' I replied. 'Emma does.'

I launched the regiment of American cockroaches into the garden, and steered them to the base of the fence. Emma, meanwhile, had selected the handset for the Death Squadron, but had not yet released the hornets from their jar.

'Hold on, here comes Dick,' she said suddenly, as the sound of Dick Cadwallader shouting at the twins burst through on audio.

'Hoi, you two! What've I told you about swimming in there! Now get the hell out before I flatten you! Y'hear?'

Dick strode across the courtyard and stood at the edge of the pool with his hands on his hips. Shaun and Ian clambered out beside him, and began towelling down.

'Jeez, you two!' Dick went on vexedly. 'People are going to *drink* that on Saturday! Why can't you do what you're told for a change, eh?'

A look of worry passed suddenly over his face. He chewed anxiously on his moustache.

'Hey. Now tell me the truth, right? You didn't do a widdle in there, did you?'

Shaun and Ian groaned.

'C'mon, Dad!' Ian said. 'What do you take us for? We're not peasants!'

'Yeah, Dad,' Shaun echoed. 'We're not like the Judges.'

Dick roared with laughter. The twins had a good giggle too. Mum gasped and put her hand up to her mouth.

'Don't worry about that, boys,' Dick said, and clapped his arms around both his sons affectionately.

'You could never be like the Judges. You've got too much breeding. Too much class. You'll never turn into losers like they are, not with *my* blood running in your veins.'

Mum shook her head, aghast. A floorboard creaked behind me as Dad stepped forward and leant down.

'So what's this surprise you've got for them, Emma?' he asked.

'It's coming, it's coming,' Emma replied.

'You should've seen the look on Louise Judge's face when I told her I wanted to buy their house!' Dick went on. 'You could've bottled it! It was a corker!'

'We did see it, Dad,' Shaun said wearily. 'We were there.'

'Hey? Oh, right. 'Course you were.' Dick cleared his throat. 'You were riding those . . . those whatch-amacallits of yours. Those billy-karts.'

'Go-karts, Dad,' Ian said.

'Go-karts, yeah, right. Anyway, I'll bet by now Louise and Pat have decided to accept my offer, poor saps. After all, they've got no choice, have they? They've had no other offers on that miserable roach-infested dump of theirs. Not since I paid every real estate agent in Dagenham a thousand bucks to un-officially take it off their books! *Ha ha ha ha ha!*'

He roared with laughter again and slapped his thigh loudly. My parents looked at each other, flabbergasted. Mum's face flushed with anger as the meaning of Dick Cadwallader's comments sunk in.

'He's been bribing the real estate agents!' she muttered finally under her breath. 'How *dare* he!'

'Emma, if you're going to do something, you better do it,' Dad said. 'Otherwise I might have to take matters into my own hands.'

Emma nodded. It was time to act. To me she said, 'I'll take the ground troops. You take the Death Squadron. But save it right till the end, till I give the order. Okay?'

'Affirmative, Commander,' I said.

Emma released the hornets out the window. I kept them in direct line of sight until they passed over the Cadwalladers' fence, then took them straight up in a giant loop-the-loop. I ran to my screen and brought them out of the loop-the-loop as they came down again.

I locked them into a holding pattern above the courtyard, while Emma took the cockroaches over the wall.

'Watch on Camera One, you'll see them come,' she said to Mum and Dad. 'Sort of like a stain . . . a big brown stain, flowing down the inside of the fence . . . Here they come now, right there . . . You see them?'

'Oh, yuck!' Mum said. 'Oh, that's disgusting! It sends shivers right down my spine!'

'Imagine them swarming all over you, all over your hair, in your face,' Emma said. 'In your clothes, under your arms, up the back of your legs. That's what we can do to the Cadwalladers. Any time we like.'

Mum's face was glowing. 'Really?' she said.

'You wouldn't give *me* a go at doing that, would you, Emma?' Dad asked.

I smiled then. Not just a tiddler of a smile, but a real face-splitter. I knew at that moment that everything was going to be all right. Our parents wouldn't sell to the Cadwalladers. No way.

With them on our side as well, Dick Cadwallader didn't stand a chance.

'Security breached, regiment in attack-launch position,' Emma announced, as the last of her cockroaches poured off the wall into the mulched garden running behind the pool. 'Death Squadron report in.'

'Death Squadron in attack-launch position, Commander,' I said.

'Hold your fire,' Emma ordered. 'I repeat. Hold your fire. Ground troops breaking cover—NOW!'

She switched from regiment to battalion handsets and launched her cockroaches out of the mulch at top speed. They hurtled across the deck to where Dick and Shaun and Ian were standing. She split them up.

As Dick started to run back towards the house, she got him with the second battalion. She got Shaun and Ian with the first battalion as they headed for the front gate. It was so easy with only three targets to aim at, it was almost ridiculous.

I just wished I had a battalion down there with her, so I could join in the fun.

Mum was gasping and groaning in disgust, but she

was also thoroughly enjoying herself. Dad was wearing an even bigger grin than I was. Through the audio we could hear the shouts and shrieks of the Cadwalladers. We could see the cockroaches swarming all over them on the screen.

Back and forth, around and around, Emma toyed with Dick and the twins like a cat toying with mice. Every time one of them tried to run for it, she cut them off and attacked them.

She kept them cornered at the very edge of the deck, with their backs to the pool.

'Pack animals!' Dick was moaning. 'Look at them! They're like wolves, hunting in packs!'

'Jump into the pool, Dad!' Shaun shouted. 'They won't get us there!'

'No, no, the champagne!' Dick said in alarm. 'We can't! It's for Saturday!'

Emma advanced the two battalions slowly. Dick and the twins shuffled back further, until they were teetering right on the brink. The vast seething brown carpet of cockroaches was almost touching them now. They had nowhere else to go.

With a groan, Dick turned and belly-flopped into the pool. Shaun and Ian followed him.

'Don't you drink any!' Dick bellowed to his sons. 'You drink any, you'll be in serious trouble, you hear!'

This was exactly what Emma wanted.

She launched the first battalion into the pool at full speed.

'They can swim!' Dick shrieked. 'They're coming for *us*! *Ahhhh-h-h-h!*'

Emma let the twins escape and went for Dick. A thousand cockroaches surrounded him and began climbing on his arms and shoulders. In ten seconds he was completely covered. He was *layered* with cockroaches, three and four deep. Not a single hair or speck of his skin could be seen.

He was yelling for help, thrashing his arms and splashing champagne everywhere. The cockroaches were clinging on to him like grim death.

'Careful you don't kill him,' Mum said. 'He might be an awful man and a lousy neighbour, but we don't want him to drown.'

'I won't kill him,' Emma said. 'Watch. This is a manoeuvre I've developed called "tickling". See what happens now.'

She began wiggling the trigger on her handset with her finger. Very fast, but very gently at the same time. I could only imagine what a strange mix of electrical signals that movement would be sending to the cockroaches' brains.

'Emma, what're you doing?' Mum said.

'Watch!' Emma repeated. 'It should start to work soon. Any second now—any second—*yes! There!*'

A murky, foul-looking yellow stain was beginning to spread out around Dick, into the pool.

'Oh no!' Mum gasped. 'They're urinating! Oh, Emma!' Dad and I burst out laughing.

Emma kept wiggling the trigger. The murky yellow stain grew and grew. Dick gave up trying to shake the cockroaches off and dived.

'He's gone under!' Emma said. 'Death Squadron! Prepare to commence bombing raids!'

'Aye aye, Commander!' I replied.

'Keep him in the pool! Every time he comes up for air, hit him!'

The cockroaches let go of Dick and swam to the surface. Dick kept swimming towards where Shaun and Ian were standing on the deck, ready to help pull him out. As soon as his head and shoulders broke the surface, I swooped down.

It was great. I got all three of them at once. On my first pass, eight of the twelve hornets hit their targets and began stinging.

'Ahhhh-h-h-h-h!'

'Yaaaa-AAAAH!'

'YeowwWWWWWW!—'

The screams were blood-curdling. All three Cadwalladers jumped back into the pool. They swam to the bottom and stayed there till their lungs were bursting.

When they came up for air, I hit them again.

'Not too much, Toby,' Mum said. 'We really don't want them to drown.'

'They're swallowing a fair bit of champagne, by the look of things,' Dad added. 'Champagne mixed with cockroach wee. *That* should be interesting.'

I locked the Death Squadron back into a holding pattern above the pool. The Cadwalladers had been stung enough now. Any more would be dangerous, as Mum said.

Just then, Dick's butler and the blonde personal assistant came running out of the house wielding cans of Baygon.

'Chemicals!' I shouted. 'Chemical weapons approaching! I'll try to hold them off! Get your battalion out of the pool!'

'Damn!' Emma swore. 'This'll take time! I have to find an exit ramp! Don't let them through!'

I wheeled the Death Squadron away from Dick and the twins and brought them around at full speed to attack the two intruders. The butler saw the hornets coming and sprayed. I swerved them just in time. All of them missed the deadly cloud. I brought them around to attack him from behind but he spun and sprayed again.

'They're good! They're good!' I exclaimed. 'I'm in trouble!'

'Just hold them!' Emma replied. 'That's all you have to do!'

Emma had directed her second battalion into the mulch at the back of the pool. A frond had fallen down from a palm tree. She was trying to use her cockroaches to push it into the pool. She burrowed the battalion in underneath the frond, moving it about six inches. She reversed, then burrowed in again.

Dick and the twins, meanwhile, had reached the deck, where they lay woozy from the champagne and utterly exhausted.

The butler and the blonde were still ten metres away. They had their backs to each other and were spraying madly, creating a protective shield of Baygon. Keeping this pose—and taking care not to breathe the Baygon themselves—they advanced slowly towards the edge of the pool, where Emma's battalion was floundering.

'I'm not going to lose *this* battalion,' Emma said to me grimly. 'You have to hold them, soldier. Just one more minute.'

'I'm trying, I'm trying,' I muttered. 'Maybe if I come in low—'

I brought the hornets in at knee-height, below the protective gas-shield. The butler sprayed with deadly accuracy, and I saw one of my hornets drop away. Fortunately, that same cloud of spray rose up around the blonde's face. She began coughing, and lifted a hand to shield her eyes.

I saw my chance. I turned the hornets sharply and attacked her from behind. Only two of my hornets hit the target, but that was enough.

She squealed and sprayed out blindly. This time she got the butler full in the face. The butler was also spraying at *her*, trying to stop my hornets as they came in.

Their formation was broken. They were disoriented, coughing and spluttering loudly. As I brought the Death Squadron in for another pass, they turned and sprinted for the house, spraying behind them wildly.

I got them a beauty, four or five stings each, before they shut the doors.

'Intruders have retreated!' I announced. 'I repeat—intruders have retreated! Chemical threat neutralised!'

'Well done,' Emma said with a sigh of relief. 'You saved my arse out there.'

'Emma, mind your language!' Mum growled.

Emma's second battalion had pushed the tip of the palm frond in the pool. She steered her first battalion across to it. They began to clamber out safely onto dry land.

Dick and the twins, meanwhile, were still lying in a drunken heap on the deck. They were moaning pitifully. Their skin was coming out in nasty red blotches where they'd been stung by the hornets. Dick tried to get to his feet, but dizziness overcame him and he slumped back down.

'I told you . . . not . . . to *drink* any!' he slurred, and then passed out.

18

operation judgement day

Next morning Dad took a day off work, so he could learn to operate one of our regiments. Mum needed a bit of persuading, but she decided to have a go too.

Straight after breakfast we launched five full regiments—a grand total of ten thousand cockroaches—in the backyard. Emma had two, I had two, and Dad had one. We showed him how to jump-start them, and how to park them in neutral so they wouldn't move. He took to it like a seasoned pro.

Mum started with the butterflies. By lunchtime she was happily steering around the Death Squadron (although not at full speed). At two o'clock she summoned up all her courage and took control of a battalion of German cockroaches, which she succeeded in marching back and forth across the lawn.

At three o'clock the pest exterminators arrived at the Cadwalladers'. We heard the piercing blast of the whistle, and the sound of the leader shouting '*Left!* . . . *Right!* . . . *Left!* . . . *Right!*' as they marched in through the gate.

A few minutes later a glowing orange gas cloud began to rise up slowly around the house.

'*That's it boys! Make sure of it this time!*' we heard Dick shouting from out on the road. '*Frizzle the little beggars! Burn them alive!*'

At eight o'clock the following evening the guests began arriving for Dick's next party. This was far and away the biggest party Dick had thrown. The helicopters just kept coming and coming, more than I could count.

A long line of limousines pulled up at Dick's front gate. Chauffeurs got out and held doors open for grey-haired important-looking men and their elegant wives.

A complete chamber orchestra arrived and began playing classical music on the corner of the deck.

A huge pot filled with steaming baby turtle soup was brought out and left to cool on the tables.

By nine o'clock the courtyard was packed. Every available inch of space was taken.

Viewing the scene from our command-and-control centre in Emma's bedroom, Dad (who was good at these things) estimated the crowd at three hundred.

'At *least* three hundred,' he said to us cautiously. 'More like three-fifty. That's an awful lot of people, Emma. You sure it's not too many?'

'Not if we execute the attack properly,' Emma

said. 'The main thing is not to lose control of our regiments. We need to stay around the outside of the courtyard, not get sucked into the middle like we did last time. Attack the chamber orchestra, attack the food tables. Create as much panic as we can. Attack the guests too, if you like, but make sure you get away and under cover before your regiment breaks up too badly.'

Dad nodded, clicking the trigger on his handset impatiently.

'Sounds good to me,' he said. He grinned suddenly and added, 'Commander.'

Emma turned to me next. 'Your first job is to empty out the gambling room,' she said. 'It's too dangerous to send cockroaches in there. They'll get trampled. You get everyone out, then fly back to the courtyard and watch for Baygon. Any sign of waiters with spray cans, you nail 'em. You've got two Death Squadrons now, with twelve hornets in each, so you can afford to lose a few if you have to. And any time you've got spare, help us herd the guests towards the gate.'

Emma addressed the three of us together—Mum, Dad and me.

'Our aim, as with the last operation, is to drive every last guest out onto the road,' she said. 'If we can do that again tonight, with all Dick's sponsors in attendance, I confidently predict his partying days will be over. From then on, we'll wear him down with small guerilla attacks, day after day, night after night. With luck, this will be the last major operation we ever have to launch. Let's make it a good one. Questions?'

Mum and Dad shook their heads. I raised my hand slowly.

'What's this operation called?' I asked.

Emma thought for a moment. 'Operation Judgement Day,' she said.

I thought that sounded pretty good.

Our cockroaches were already in position along the base of the Cadwalladers' fence. Dad and Emma had two handsets each. Mum had one. There would be no battalion handsets used in this attack—it would be regiments only.

Ten thousand cockroaches and twenty-four hornets against three hundred and fifty humans. The battle lines were drawn.

At Emma's command I launched the hornets out the window. Immediately afterwards she ordered the cockroaches over the wall. I sent both my squadrons up in a giant loop-the-loop above the Cadwalladers' place and raced to my position in front of the screen.

I brought up Camera One inside the gambling room. Then I checked on Camera Two—perched high up on the Cadwalladers' roof—to catch my hornets on the way down. I kept both squadrons tightly together and steered them down into the courtyard, through the double doors to the gambling room.

It wasn't a casino night. There were no games at the tables. The room was full of people chatting and drinking. I didn't want to sting anyone yet, so I began buzzing the crowd. I split my two squadrons up and guided them in and out, round about, keeping an easy cruising speed a good several inches above people's heads.

'Okay, I'm inside!' I said. 'I'm working my audience! They're getting nicely warmed up!'

'Dick's handing out champagne from the pool,' I heard Emma say to Mum. 'It looks pretty orange from all that pesticide.'

'What, you mean people are *drinking* that stuff?' Mum asked. 'Yuck!'

'Hey!' I barked. 'Are you girls going to stand there gossiping all day? Or are you going to attack?'

'Get that room emptied out first,' Emma said. 'We're in the mulch behind the pool. We'll come in right behind and secure the door.'

The crowd inside the gambling room was getting agitated. People were ducking their heads, spilling their drinks, taking swipes at my hornets as they flew past. It wasn't exactly panic, though. Nobody was rushing to get out. I was going to have to sting somebody to make that happen: there was nothing else for it.

As luck would have it, Dick Cadwallader's agent, Mitch Grinderling, stepped out of the men's room in the corner.

'Hey, Mitch!' I said in delight to the screen. 'Glad you could make it, mate! I need someone to do a bit of screaming, and it looks like you're it!'

I swung both squadrons around and let him have it. Very helpfully, he began screaming right on cue. I didn't sting him much—maybe a dozen, fifteen times, tops—and all on his arms and shoulders. Mostly I kept both squadrons hovering just above his head, so the noise of the hornets buzzing would be ringing loudly in his ears.

'We're cooking here, we're cooking!' I shouted to Mum and Dad and Emma, as panic began to set in. 'Our old mate Mitch is doing the job for us! Get ready!'

I switched from flying at head-height to flying at waist-height, which was a lot trickier. It was like piloting a jet plane through a forest in which the trees are constantly moving. I sent a squadron in to sting Mitch Grinderling on the bum, and he ran yelping out onto the deck. I doubled back to the end of the room and stung a couple more people. That was it—end of story.

Everyone ran helter-skelter for the double doors.

'They're coming out, they're coming out!' I shouted.

'We're coming in, we're coming in!' Emma shouted.

'Watch those feet!' Dad shouted.

'Keep to the outside of the courtyard!' Mum shouted.

'Secure the door, then head for the chamber orchestra!' Emma shouted. 'Head for the food tables! Cha-a-a-arge!'

From that point on, it was wild. Somehow I managed to keep my hornets in sight, and keep them buzzing just above the heads of the crowd. How Emma and Mum and Dad managed to keep sight of their cockroaches, I'll never know.

At one point, out of the corner of my eye, I saw someone's regiment climbing up the wall of the garage.

At another point I saw a regiment swarming over the fountain in the middle of the pool.

I saw one guest try to climb up one of the sun-umbrellas and bring the whole lot—table and all—crashing to the ground.

I saw another guest jump onto a food table, then, when a regiment of cockroaches came up after him, he jumped *right into the steaming pot of baby turtle soup*.

I saw champagne glasses smashing everywhere.

I saw men and women leaping into each other's arms.

I saw a violinist from the chamber orchestra whacking at cockroaches with her violin.

Finally I saw Dick Cadwallader and half a dozen waiters come out of the double doors holding cans of Baygon.

Dick was in a towering rage. His face was purple. He launched himself at any cockroaches he could see, spraying madly. I sent a squadron of hornets down to attack him, and managed to push him back, but as soon as my hornets flew away from him, he came again.

Meanwhile the other waiters had spread out. They'd realised that there were only two squadrons of hornets, and those two squadrons couldn't be everywhere at once. I raced around the courtyard at top speed, stinging as many waiters as I could, but I'm sad to say they did spray an alarming number of cockroaches.

Fortunately, they also sprayed an alarming number of guests. That was what finally turned the tide of the battle in our favour.

It was Dick and his waiters who drove their own guests out to the road.

That, combined with some clever tactics from Emma, and some disciplined teamwork from Mum, Dad and me.

At the end, shortly after a quarter to ten, the entire pool deck was covered in a haze of Baygon. It hung over the courtyard like a fog, making it very difficult for people to breathe. Only Dick remained inside the fence, a wild-eyed, dishevelled figure, spitting curses and waving his spray-can at the shadows. The music had long since stopped, but the beams from the search-lights on the roof danced all around him, making him look still crazier and more wild-eyed than he already was.

All of our cockroach regiments had got out safely. We'd suffered casualties, yes, but nothing like as many as in our previous operation. Emma had kept her own American regiments till last, creating a diversion near the double doors which allowed Mum and Dad to take their Germans back over the fence behind the pool.

Like any good commander, Emma led from the front. She did all the most difficult jobs herself. Only when it became clear that the last of the guests were leaving did she bring her own troops home.

I still had my hornets in a holding pattern, high above the haze of Baygon. Our butterflies were safe above the haze too. All five of them had survived.

Through the audio on Camera Four near the front gate, we could hear the groans of the guests out on the footpath. They weren't groaning because of hornet stings—very few of them had been stung this time. They were groaning because they'd inhaled Dick Cadwallader's Baygon, or drunk some of his polluted champagne.

It was another famous victory. Dick's reputation as a party host was in ruins. There would be no more horrible, noisy parties every Wednesday and Saturday. All that remained now was to make sure we hounded him into a full and total surrender.

With this on our minds we flew the hornets and the butterflies out of the battle zone to join the rest of our insect army in the backyard.

19

too easy

We all had a cup of Milo in the kitchen before we went to bed. It was so nice to have some peace and quiet on a Saturday night, it seemed a shame to waste it. Instead of sleeping, we just wanted to sit there at the table and listen.

'I must say,' Mum said to Dad proudly, 'I knew we had clever kids, but I didn't know they were *this* clever. To attack Dick Cadwallader with an army of remote-controlled insects! I never would've thought of that in a million years!'

'Yeah, well, they get all their cleverness from *me*, of course,' Dad said, and winked at us. 'It's no wonder they're both such geniuses.'

'Emma's the real genius,' I said. 'It was her idea about the insects. I'm just the grunt who takes the orders.'

'No, no, Toby, not at all!' Mum protested. 'The way you flew those hornets tonight was nothing short of spectacular! I'd say you've got a definite future as a fighter pilot.'

'You weren't so bad yourself, Lou,' Dad put in. 'For a woman who hates cockroaches.'

'Yeah, Mum,' Emma echoed. 'I reckon you're a natural. I'll have to give you your own battalion for Christmas.'

We laughed for a while and finished our Milos. Just before we went to bed, Mum said to us, 'You know, the one person I really feel sorry for is Beverly Cadwallader. That poor woman's been ill since the day she won the money. She's never got to enjoy a cent of it. And I'll bet if she'd been well all this time, she never would've let Dick behave so badly.'

'No, she would've kept him on the straight and narrow, that's for sure,' Dad said. 'None of this nonsense with the new house would've happened if Bev had been around.'

'I can't help thinking Dick's not doing enough to make her better, either,' Mum went on. 'He's looking after her well enough, I'm not worried about that. With the nurse in the house I'm sure she gets all the care she needs. But he needs to try some different therapies. When I was working as a nurse and we had to deal with this sort of thing, I found that a good fright sometimes cured it. I'm not saying Dick should use drugs or electric shock treatment, or anything like that. But people who regress to childhood are hiding from something. They're acting like babies because they can't cope.

They need a good jolt to bring them back into the real world.'

Dad put his empty mug down on the bench and gazed at Mum in admiration.

'How come you know so much about this?' he said. 'I didn't know you'd had any patients with a mental age of one and a half.'

'Sure I did.' Mum elbowed him in the ribs. 'I married one.'

She ran off, squealing and giggling, as Dad chased her all the way down the hall.

The following night, Emma sent a battalion of German cockroaches over to Dick's house on a special raid.

It was eleven o'clock. The last light in the Cadwalladers' house had just gone out. We had our five butterfly-cams located in a line leading from the security fence right up to Dick's bedroom.

Operation Judgement Day was entering its second phase.

It took Emma less than five minutes to get her cockroaches to the bedroom, from the time they went over the wall. Camera One took them across the courtyard to the stairs. Camera Two took them up the first flight. Camera Three took them across the hall to the second. Camera Four took them up onto the third storey, and Camera Five took her right to Dick's door.

By the time they arrived I'd brought Camera One in from outside. Camera One was our smallest butterfly and the only one that could fit under Dick's door.

I flew it down gently but missed, twice. The first time I bonked it against the wood. The second time I bonked it against the floor.

'You're getting up to your old tricks again,' Emma grumbled.

'Hey, give me a chance,' I said. 'The gap at the base of that door can't be more than a centimetre wide.'

The fifth time I flew it down, I got it exactly into the gap. I hit the trigger sharply, giving it a quick burst of speed, and it was through. With the aid of the camera I looked briefly around the room, and finally chose to perch on top of the window, facing Dick's bed.

Dick was fast asleep and snoring loudly. The bedspread was pulled up over his chest and tucked under his arms.

'This is too easy,' Emma said. 'Look at him. It's like taking candy from a baby.'

With a dry, pattering, rustling sound, her battalion of cockroaches poured in under the door.

They marched to the bed and climbed up onto it.

A thousand of them covered the bedspread from top to bottom.

The front-line cockroaches had advanced as far as Dick's neck. Emma stopped them just as their antennae began tickling his chin. Dick chuckled in his sleep, then turned on his side, opening a gap between the sheets just in front of him.

'Mmm, darling,' Dick mumbled, smiling dreamily and puckering his lips for an imaginary kiss. 'Mmmm, yes. Oh, yes—'

Emma steered her cockroaches right into the gap between the sheets. They burrowed as far down into the bed as they could, next to Dick.

Then Emma switched her handset off and let them run free.

Dick tossed and turned. He grunted. He groaned. He jerked his legs this way and that. He lay perfectly still on his back for a second, then his eyes opened as wide as saucers.

He leapt up, bellowing at the top of his voice, and hurled his cockroach-infested bedspread halfway across the room.

Mum and Dad and I cheered and clapped. Emma gave a short bow, then jumped her cockroaches back into formation and retreated quickly. By the time Dick had got up to turn on the light and retrieve his bedspread, the entire battalion had vanished under the door.

After that, we worked in shifts. Mum took a battalion of Americans in just after midnight, and woke Dick up a second time. Dad took another battalion of Americans in at two a.m. Just before four, I took a Death Squadron in, and buzzed Dick right out of his bedroom and down the hall.

As expected, Dick's butler and personal assistant came at the squadron with cans of Baygon, but I avoided them easily. As a seasoned veteran of two major combat operations, plus a number of minor skirmishes, I could handle two amateurs with spray-cans, no worries.

The following day was Monday, the end of the holidays. Shaun and Ian went back to boarding school. Dad went to work as usual. For Emma and me, it was a pupil-free day, which meant we could stay at home.

Emma sent another battalion of cockroaches over to the Cadwalladers at ten o'clock. She found Dick asleep on the couch in the living room. She steered her cockroaches up the side of the mantelpiece and knocked over all the ornaments above the fireplace, smashing them one by one.

The language Dick used, as he chased Emma's cockroaches back down the stairs, was so bad I had to turn the audio off. If I'd listened to him swearing any longer, it would've melted my ears.

We kept up this guerilla campaign, mostly at night, for a week. On Wednesday Dick went to sleep with half a dozen cans of Baygon next to his bed—which didn't stop us from waking him up again, although it meant we couldn't exactly stick around and have a chat with him afterwards.

On Thursday night Dick posted his butler outside the bedroom door on sentry duty. The butler was wearing a full-body hooded protective suit and a gasmask. He had a spray-pack of orange pesticide on his back, ready to shoot at anything that came near.

I sent both my Death Squadrons in to get him. One went on a suicide mission to draw his fire. The other aimed at his neck and swooped in under his hood.

I lost eight out of twelve hornets in the suicide squad. They got hit by the orange pesticide spray and simply dissolved in mid-air. The hornets under the hood did the job for us, however. They stung that butler so badly that he ripped his hood off, dropped his spray-pack on the floor, and flung himself down the stairs.

A few minutes later we heard the sound of an engine starting, and a car driving off into the night.

On Friday night the house was empty, except for Beverly Cadwallader and her nurse. On Saturday morning Dick reappeared and hammered a giant FOR SALE sign into the grass outside his front gate.

Emma saw the sign first. She'd gone down to the shop for Mum, to buy milk and vegetables, and caught Dick banging it in as she returned. I was out in the backyard with Mum and Dad, showing them some of the finer points of hornet-flying, when Emma came sprinting around the corner of the house.

'Mum! Dad! Dick's putting a sign up! He's selling! He's selling! Come see!'

I quickly flew the hornets back into their jar. We hurried up the drive to take a look. Dick finished hammering just as we arrived, and was preparing to go inside again. He paused as we approached him and scowled at us. He was unshaven and unwashed. His fly was undone, and all his shirt-buttons had been done up in the wrong holes.

'You selling up, Dick?' Dad asked innocently. 'Jee, that's a shame.'

'Sooner I get out of this dump the better,' Dick grumbled, jerking a thumb at his house. 'Infested with cockroaches. And hornets, too. I've tried everything, but I can't get rid of them. Had to book myself into a hotel last night, just to get some shut-eye. They're making my life a bloody misery.'

He sniffed despondently, then pointed to our own FOR SALE sign, visible behind some shrubs on our front lawn.

'That must be why you're selling too, is it?' he said. 'Pests?'

Dad smiled at him sweetly. 'No, we've got rid of ours.'

On our way back, Mum and Dad and Emma and I pulled our FOR SALE sign out of the ground and carried it down the drive to the garage.

20

the final mission

We went out to dinner the following night, to our favourite Italian restaurant, to celebrate.

Dad got sentimental while we were eating dessert. He decided to make a speech.

He got awkwardly to his feet and tapped his spoon on his glass for quiet, then cleared his throat, brushed some crumbs of garlic bread off his shirt, and smiled.

'We are gathered here today—' he began.

'Good grief, Patrick, it's not a funeral!' Mum cut in. 'You sound like a priest!'

'You forgot to say "Dearly beloved", Dad,' Emma added.

She and Mum snickered quietly together. Dad looked hurt.

'Listen,' he said. 'This may not be the best speech in the world, and I may never be Secretary General of the United Nations, but it's my speech, and I'd appreciate a few less interruptions.'

Mum and Emma looked solemn.

'Sorry,' Mum said.

'In the long and distinguished history of the Judge family,' Dad went on, 'there has never been a day like this. Years from now, when your mum and I have got grandkids and great-grandkids, and we're so old we can't eat properly anymore and we have to suck mashed potato through a straw, we'll sit by the fire and tell the story of how Emma and Toby defeated Dick Cadwallader in the famous Battle of St Clairs Road.

'We'll remember that it was you two brave souls who kept the fires of hope burning when all seemed lost,' Dad went on. 'When your mother and I were desperate and demoralised, you two never gave up.'

Dad paused. He picked up his glass of water and held it out in front of him.

'And so, without further ado, I'd like to propose a toast,' he said. 'To me, Patrick Judge, for being such an all-round brilliant bloke.'

'*What?*' Emma said.

'Just kidding, just kidding,' Dad grinned. 'To Toby and Emma. The best kids any dad could want.'

Mum raised her glass and clinked it against Dad's.

'To Toby and Emma,' she echoed.

'And to 388 St Clairs Road, Dagenham,' Dad added. 'Our home.'

'Actually, I'm getting pretty sick of Dagenham,' Mum sighed. 'I think I'd like to sell.'

We all stared at her.

'Just kidding, just kidding,' Mum said.

Emma and I pelted her with garlic bread crusts. Dad emptied a whole glass of iced water down the back of her neck, while Emma and I held her arms.

We had one more mission left to accomplish, before we disbanded our victorious cockroach army.

This was a mercy mission. To save Beverly Cadwallader.

On Sunday morning after breakfast, Emma and I launched a battalion each. We took them up over the fence, in through the double doors, and up two flights of stairs to the third floor.

The Cadwalladers' house was deserted. As we approached Beverly's door, however, we heard a muffled voice talking inside.

'That's the nurse,' Emma said. 'We'll have to get her out first. We need to deal with Beverly on her own.'

'Please don't be changing her nappy,' I muttered. 'Please, please—'

I parked my battalion and flew Camera One in under the door. I perched on a bookshelf in the corner, and surveyed the room.

To my great relief, the nurse wasn't changing Beverly's nappy. She was seated on a chair next to an enormous cot, reading Beverly a story.

Beverly was sitting cross-legged at the nurse's feet. Blocks and soft toys and alphabet puzzles lay strewn on the floor all around her. She was gazing rapturously at some brightly coloured pictures of trains in a book that the nurse was holding up.

'Choo-choo!' she said. 'Me want more choo-choo!'

'No Beverly, not again.' The nurse shook her head. 'I've already read it six times this morning. And besides, it's nearly time for your nap.'

'No nap!' Beverly said firmly. 'Choo-choo!'

'Yes nap, you little cutie!' The nurse bent down and pinched Beverly's cheek. 'Aren't you just the sweetest thing? Aren't you just cute as a button?'

Beverly giggled contentedly. She sat down, picked up a block and began sucking on it. Then she saw Emma's cockroach battalion flooding under the door.

'Ooooooooooo!' she said.

The nurse turned, then gasped when she saw the cockroaches. They advanced further into the room and halted. I brought mine in behind them and veered sharply off to the right, towards the wall.

The nurse didn't move. She didn't say a word. She stared at Emma's cockroaches with one hand pressed to her chest, breathing hard.

Emma jumped them. A thousand cockroaches leapt a metre into the air. Beverly giggled in delight and clapped her hands.

'Wheeeeeeeeeeeeee!' she said. 'Yump! Yump!'

The nurse gave a strangled shriek and ran from the room.

'Now, quick, before she comes back!' Emma hissed at me. 'Go!'

I marched my battalion right up to Beverly Cadwallader. She wasn't afraid. She picked up one of my front-line cockroaches and held it up to her face.

'Thweetie!' she said. 'Yum yum!'

She opened her mouth wide and bit its head off.

'Hey! Stop that!' I jammed my finger on the trigger, launching the rest of my battalion in a full-speed attack. Cockroaches swarmed over Beverly's bare tree-trunk legs and onto her nappy. From there they climbed up through the folds of her T-shirt and onto her shoulders.

Beverly laughed. She thought it was great fun. She picked another cockroach off her lap and bit the head off that one too.

'If you want to eat them, then eat them!' I shouted. 'Here they come!'

I sent the cockroaches surging up onto Beverly's face. She didn't like that at all. She wailed and began swatting them off, squashing them against her cheeks with her hands. She opened her mouth to cry out, but it immediately filled with cockroaches. She spat half a dozen onto the floor, but another half-dozen crawled in to replace them.

She stood up.

She began swatting, shaking, kicking, squashing,

slapping, punching and mangling my battalion to smithereens.

'Reinforcements!' I shouted.

'On the way!' Emma shouted back. 'Boy, she's a mean critter this one! Hold on!'

Beverly staggered around the room, puffing and grunting with exertion. Emma's battalion came in behind her and swarmed up the backs of her legs. She twisted and turned, but she couldn't get them off her. They raced up between her shoulder blades and buried themselves in her hair.

'Dick!' Beverly squealed. 'Dick, help! Get them off me-e-e-e-e!'

Emma punched the air in delight and gave me a quick high-five. 'We've done it, soldier, we've done it!' she said. 'Don't stop now!'

'Dick, Dick! Where are you?' Beverly went on. '*Di-i-i-i-ick!*'

The nurse appeared in the doorway holding a can of Baygon. When she saw Beverly standing there, shouting for her husband, she stopped dead.

'Who are you?' Beverly demanded. 'And where's Dick? Whose house is this anyway?'

The nurse reeled backwards. She dropped her can of Baygon onto the floor. For the second time in five minutes, she ran shrieking from the room.

The Cadwalladers' house sold later that same week. It was bought by a very nice family—the Knights—who have six kids. The kids all go to Dagenham West State School, and Dagenham High. I've become good mates with the youngest, Joey. The middle boy, Ben, asked Emma out on a date recently, but she said no, she was too busy with her experiments.

One day soon she'll be a famous scientist. Her work with remote-controlled insects will be known all over the world.

The Knights make a bit of noise sometimes, like any neighbours. But they don't own a helicopter. They don't turn their music up too loud. They've turned Dick's helipad into a skateboard ramp. Joey and I go up there a couple of times a week to practise our moves.

The house is still ugly, but at least it isn't painted bright red anymore. It's a very pleasant shade of light green.

We disbanded all our armed forces the day after the Cadwalladers' house got sold. It was a very sad occasion. We let the hornets and butterflies go first, out the window of Emma's bedroom. Then we stacked all our plastic buckets full of cockroaches in the boot and on the trailer, and Dad drove them back to the *Mirror Sun* warehouse in town.

We carried the buckets in through the back way, via the loading bay. Emma unloaded her American cockroaches first and held them in formation. I unloaded the Germans and marched them in behind.

The survivors from all five regiments lined up together on the warehouse floor.

'Cockroaches!' Emma said, when everything was quiet. 'The Judge family of Dagenham owes you a great debt! In our hour of need you came to our aid and performed great deeds of valour! It is time now for you to return to your families and to your life here among the paper reels in the *Mirror Sun* warehouse. But we will not forget you. The memory of your brave service will live forever in our minds. And nor will we forget your many, many hundreds of brave comrades who made the ultimate sacrifice and lost their lives in defence of our home.'

Emma bowed her head for a moment. 'I ask now that we observe a minute's silence in honour of fallen comrades,' she said.

Dad took off his hat. We all stood at attention, our hands clasped in our laps.

'Thank you,' Emma said when the minute was up. 'Now could we raise our handsets please.'

Mum and Dad and I raised our handsets. 'Cockroaches, live long and prosper!' Emma said.

'Handsets off!'

We switched off our handsets. There was a split second of dusty stillness in the dimly-lit warehouse. Then cockroaches scattered in all directions. Thousands of them darted and scampered across the concrete, swarming over and under and around each other in their rush towards the shelves.

Within a minute, the warehouse floor was deserted. Our valiant, victorious cockroach army was gone.

We drove home from town in an easy, contented silence. The empty trailer rattled and banged behind the car. Halfway up Dagenham Road, Dad reached across and squeezed Mum's knee.

'A cockroach for your thoughts, my love,' he said.

Mum grinned at him. 'I was just thinking how disgusting they are,' she said. 'If I saw one in my kitchen a minute after we got home, I'd spray it, quick as a wink.'

'Maybe you ought to try eating them, like Beverly did,' Emma suggested.

'No, thank you very much. That's one method of pest extermination I'll *never* try.'

'Have you heard from Beverly since she got better, Mum?' I asked.

'Yes, we had coffee together yesterday,' Mum answered. 'She's still pretty upset about all the terrible things Dick did while she was sick. She can't apologise enough. But she told me Dick's a changed man since she recovered. He's lost the urge to spend so much money. He's going to sell all his extra cars and all his speedboats, and just keep one helicopter. He's dropped the assault charges against your father and he's even talking about giving a large donation to charity, which must be a first.'

'What about Shaun and Ian?' I asked. 'Will they still go to Waldorf's?'

'No, not for a while at least,' Mum said. 'They've started at a state school across town. Beverly said it's important that they stop being such horrible spoiled brats. If they do well at their new school, and get on with the kids there, they can have the choice to go back to Waldorf's later on.'

As soon as we arrived home we stacked the handsets and empty plastic buckets in the cupboard in the garage. We were all just about to go inside when Dad stopped. He turned to Emma thoughtfully.

'Tell me something, Commander,' he said. 'Those microchip receivers. They're still inside the cockroaches' heads, right?'

'Sure, Dad,' Emma nodded. 'There was no need to take them out. Once they're switched off, the cockroaches don't even know they're there.'

'So I could go back to the warehouse with a handset, at any time, and round them up again?'

Emma shrugged. 'As long as they're still alive,' she said. 'You could catch more hornets and butterflies, too. It doesn't take long. But why would you want to do that?'

'Oh, no reason.' Dad winked at us, and gave us a sly, mysterious grin. 'It's just nice to know we can do it, that's all. In case we have problems with any of our *other* neighbours . . .'

JONATHAN HARLEN was born in New Zealand but now lives in coastal New South Wales, near Byron Bay, with his wife and three young children. He runs a small farm, where he grows coffee beans and cabinet timbers. He has published many books in various genres and for various age groups. They include the much-acclaimed young adult novel, *The Lion and the Lamb*, *Fireflies* (also for young adults), and *Brain Scam* and *Circus Berzerkus* (for younger readers).